Cold Grab

Cold Grab

Steven Barwin

James Lorimer & Company Ltd., Publishers
Toronto

James Lorimer & Company Ltd., Publishers acknowledges funding support from the Ontario Arts Council (OAC), an agency of the Government of Ontario. We acknowledge the support of the Canada Council for the Arts, which last year invested $153 million to bring the arts to Canadians throughout the country. This project has been made possible in part by the Government of Canada and with the support of Ontario Creates.

Cover design: Tyler Cleroux
Cover image: Shutterstock

978-1-4594-1381-8
eBook also available 978-1-4594-1380-1

Cataloguing data available from Library and Archives Canada.

Published by:
James Lorimer &
Company Ltd., Publishers
117 Peter Street, Suite 304
Toronto, ON, Canada
M5V 0M3
www.lorimer.ca

Distributed in the US by:
Lerner Publisher Services
1251 Washington Ave. N.
Minneapolis, MN, USA
55401
www.lernerbooks.com

Printed and bound in Canada.
Manufactured by Friesens Corporation in Altona, Manitoba, Canada in May 2019.
Job #255151

*Every year thousands of Filipino teens
are brought by their mothers to live in Canada.
This is one story . . .*

Chapter 1

Bago (New)

Through the glass, Angelo watched a blur of people go by. All he wanted was to be home. Home was eleven time zones away in the Philippines.

He sighed heavily and pressed his head against the bus window. Then he closed his eyes, shutting out the world he was forced to be in.

In his mind, he replaced the grey city with bright blue skies, towering white clouds, and a turquoise sea. He saw himself sitting in a worn,

wooden bangca fishing boat, bobbing in the
South China Sea. His grandfather, Paolo, sat
in the back, steering the small motor. Angelo
turned to look at Paolo, whose windblown hair
and face was weathered from a lifetime in the
sun. Paolo turned his gaze back to the horizon.
He knew these waters like the back of his hand.

Bamboo outriggers to their left and right
steadied their ride as they broke through the
wake. On the narrow boat, Angelo held a
fishing line in his hands. He was excited to
catch some goatfish and maybe even some
grouper. Everything he knew about fishing was
from Paolo. Angelo could feel the line with its
baited hook running through his hands as he
fed it out to sea. He looked up at the bright
light of the sun. Suddenly, it turned red.

Angelo opened his eyes to see the glare of
tail lights from a truck out the window. The
truck moved on and Angelo caught a glimpse
of himself reflected in the glass. He had dark
skin and was short like his grandfather, with

broad shoulders. His thick, black hair looked windblown even when there wasn't a breeze. Angelo smirked at the reflection of the kid looking back at him and huddled in his winter jacket.

Angelo glanced at Yvonne. He remembered a different version of his mother, one with blacker hair, one who could outrun him. "This is our stop," she said. She got up and clutched her purse. The bus rattled to a jagged stop. "Come on."

Angelo's head felt heavy as he lifted it off the window and got up. Walking down the stairs and out into the loud chaos of the city street, he wondered where exactly he was. Angelo muttered to Yvonne in Tagalog that he was cold.

"English, please," she demanded. She wanted him to speak the language of this land.

It had been a long time since Angelo had seen Yvonne. Almost ten years, to be exact. He was just a young boy when she took off from their home in Cagayan de Oro in the province of Mindanao. First, she went to Hong Kong for work, then Dubai. She had been in Canada for the last five years.

Angelo frowned at the woman he hardly knew and said, "Whatever." He followed her along a busy sidewalk lined with people moving in a rush. They passed a gas station, a grocery store, a bakery, and a Malaysian restaurant. Angelo wondered if the food there tasted like home. He looked up. All of the buildings except for the gas station had apartments on top.

They approached a white-brick, two-storey building. A sign showed an image of the CN Tower next to the words *Filipino Centre, Toronto*.

Yvonne held the door open for Angelo. "Why we here?" he asked.

She didn't answer. As it was, he knew the answer. But how could this place make anything about life in cold Canada better?

He held his ground until she pulled him inside. "*Hay naku?*" he asked.

"English," Yvonne demanded.

"Why do I have to do this?"

She didn't answer.

Their appointment was with a woman named Marijean. She carried a clipboard and had long, black hair. "Welcome to Toronto, Canada, Angelo. How are you?" she said, showing a big smile.

Angelo didn't respond. He kept his eyes aimed at the floor.

"Don't be rude," Yvonne said, gently nudging him.

Marijean smiled. "It's okay Ms. Torres, don't worry about it. It takes time to adjust. I've been here almost ten years, and I'm still figuring things out. That's just what we all have to go through." She turned back to him. "The important thing is that you are finally here, Angelo! Your mother has told me so much about you."

Mother? he thought. A mother was someone who took care of her child. Someone who protected them, stayed with them. The woman beside Angelo? All she was to him was Yvonne.

Chapter 2

Pinoy (Filipino)

Angelo trailed behind during Marijean's tour.

"So we opened up more than seventeen years ago to help people adjust to life here. This whole building is ours. The floor we are on is rented out to stores and services. Upstairs we have doctors, lawyers, accountants. Pretty much anything any Filipino-Canadian could need."

Angelo looked around. He wasn't impressed.

Marijean smiled and said to Angelo, "But the floor that you're going to be most interested in is downstairs. Follow me."

They took the stairs to the lower level, which was set up as a community centre. Angelo was shown classrooms and a gym where younger kids were playing basketball. The last stop was the library.

He wasn't interested in playing basketball or joining the line-dancing club. He cared even less that there was a room filled with Filipino books, even though it seemed like a big deal to Marijean.

She rattled on. "I was telling your mom that after school, you can come here for homework help. Our Pinoy tutors are University of Toronto students. Oh, I should ask, have you started school yet?"

He nodded to avoid a jab from Yvonne.

"Well, we give out academic awards. Who knows? Maybe you can win some scholarships. Come have a seat here."

She sat Angelo at a table in front of a book all about Canada. He grimaced at the polar bear on the front cover. Around him, other Filipino students were studying.

Marijean asked a boy sitting at the same table how long he'd been in Canada.

Angelo turned to him. He looked about the same age as Angelo, but he had more scruff above his lip.

"No, let me guess," Marijean said. "Two months."

"Close. Five," the boy said.

Like she would've got a prize or something, thought Angelo.

"Name's Marcus Ramos," said the boy. "Grade eleven."

"Same grade as you, Angelo!" Yvonne piped up with excitement.

Marijean pulled Yvonne away, leaving Angelo with awkward silence to fill. He was about to turn away when Marcus looked up from his book.

"Pretty crappy here, huh?"

Angelo's curiosity was piqued, but he didn't respond.

"The snow looks cool in online pictures," Marcus scoffed. "Good from far, but far from good." He laughed too loudly. When other students shushed him, he scowled back at them.

Angelo smiled. The smile was his first since stepping onto the plane at Ninoy Aquino International Airport in Manila.

Marcus stood. "Anyway, hang in there. You'll be all hockey, doughnuts, and wrestling polar bears in no time." He laughed out loud again before leaving.

Angelo noticed that the book on Canadian history Marcus was looking at was still on the table. He reached for it and saw something underneath. Hidden under the book was a magazine: *Tiger Beat — the hottest source for breaking news and gossip on teen celebs.* The page was open to pictures of Taylor Swift.

Angelo smiled again.

✱✱✱

Angelo made his way outside through the front doors. Yvonne was waiting for him. "Looks like you made your first friend."

Angelo shrugged. If he had any respect for Yvonne, he might have responded.

At home, in their small apartment on the fifteenth floor, Angelo sat on a fold-out futon. He tried to focus on the dialogue on TV. Who knew that watching TV could be considered work? It was his history teacher's idea that watching TV could help Angelo improve his understanding of North America. But keeping up with the fast-paced talk and strange references made him lose interest. His other homework was to read for half an hour. At his side was a bowl from dinner and the book about Canada.

"Clean up when you're done. And don't go to bed too late. You've got school tomorrow," Yvonne said as she moved to her bedroom. Before closing the door, she added, "I clean all day. So don't think I'm going to clean up after you. 'Night."

It's weird that she shares the apartment with another woman, Angelo thought. The woman they shared the place with was also from the Philippines, also a housekeeper. Angelo knew his mom couldn't afford an extra bedroom for him. He looked around the tiny two-bedroom place. Every piece of furniture, he was told, was either a street find or from a donation place. He thought about pulling the futon out into a bed. He wondered who owned it before. No bedroom. Zero privacy. He was told to be thankful about having a roof over his head.

As he flicked through channels, his eyelids became heavy. He slouched lower and lower. *The only good thing about sleep*, he thought, *is that I can escape the new life I am trapped in and dream of home*. The bright blue skies, towering white clouds, and clear turquoise seas.

Chapter 3

Paaralan (School)

Angelo woke to silence. He needed both hands to prop himself up, and he had fallen asleep in his clothes. He felt something under his leg and fished out the welcome to Canada book that he had failed to read. His history teacher was not going to be happy.

In the kitchen, Angelo rummaged for breakfast. It took a few tries before he found where the cups and cutlery were. It seemed that millions of little things were brand new to him and he had to figure them all out one by one. He decided on a bread roll and slice of cheese.

He took a bite and opened his book to a random page. He read several facts about Canada.

- Canada is the second-largest country in the world next to Russia.
- Canada has more lakes than the rest of the world combined.
- Canadians eat more macaroni and cheese than any other country in the world.

Angelo looked forward to trying that dish.

- When bodies of water freeze in winter, Canadians like to play hockey on them.

Angelo flipped the page. He read that the North American beaver was Canada's national symbol. And that Canada was an Iroquoian word, meaning "village." *What is an Iroquoian?*

he wondered.

As he shut the book, he remembered the note from Yvonne sitting on the kitchen table. She was always up and out before the sun every day except for Sunday, church day. She left a note to encourage him.

Smile. My world is better with you in it. And brush your teeth.

Angelo crumpled the note. He tossed it out before he showered and changed. He took the stairs, all fifteen flights, down. He had learned that one elevator was always out of service and the other was too busy in the morning rush. Some mornings, like that day, even the stairs were backed up with people leaving the building.

Finally, he was on the main level and through the double doors. He shivered in the cold. The change between inside and outside was too extreme. He walked and watched with amazement as cars drove on the snow and slippery ice. It reminded him of his father's job, driving trucks during the wet and mud of the rainy seasons back home. His dad had always been on the road. Mud would slide down from the hillsides and just swallow up cars. Then one night, Angelo was woken by a knock on the door. He didn't have to listen in on his grandfather's discussion with the police to know what had happened. After that, Yvonne's father Paolo had taken care of Angelo and his big brother, Carlos.

Yvonne sent as much money as she could to help out. But Angelo knew that money could never replace love. Just like a phone call couldn't replace being there.

When Angelo left the Philippines, it meant saying goodbye to Paolo and Carlos. Carlos was over eighteen, so coming to Canada was not an option because their mother couldn't sponsor him. Plus, he had his own family — a wife and a newborn baby — to take care of. If Carlos was here, Angelo thought, things would be a little better.

✵ ✵ ✵

The high school loomed over Angelo in the cement jungle that was the city. The big building didn't just look old. It *was* old. In front, students listened to music on their phones and played basketball. To Angelo, it looked like everyone was smoking. But it was just steam rising from their mouths, as warm air brushed against cold air.

Angelo squeezed past a couple who were making out. In Cagayan de Oro, the school had a strict policy against students dating. Posted signs and assemblies always reminded students that relationships could end up destroying the future of young ladies.

The bell rang loudly. Angelo dropped off his jacket and backpack at his locker. In his first class, he took a seat in the back row. He kept his hoodie over his head because even inside felt cold. The second period teacher was stricter. She made him pull his hood down and demanded to see homework. The morning crawled by as Angelo played up his broken

English to get out of working.

Out in the hallway, the lunchtime crowd was on the move. He turned left and realized he was going the wrong way, the way that wouldn't get him to the cafeteria. Halfway through a U-turn, he felt a thud against him. He recoiled.

"Hey, watch where you are going!"

Angelo cowered away. He didn't lift his eyes to look at the person he ran into.

"What's wrong with you? Don't talk?"

The last thing Angelo needed was a fight.

"You *bobo*?"

What? Bobo was Tagalog for "stupid." Angelo looked up. Staring back was a dark-skinned boy with his hair buzzed short. He wore a tank top showing off a tattoo of the sun from the Philippines flag.

"Hey, I know this guy," another voice said. Marcus stepped toward Angelo. "Angelo, this is Felix. He's just giving you a hard time." He pointed at another Filipino boy behind Felix. "And this is Darius."

Darius was tall and thin and he had thick, messy hair. "Let's roll."

"We're heading out," Marcus said. "Come on, Angelo."

Angelo didn't know what to do. Were they just messing with him?

"Come on!"

Angelo followed them down the hallway. It felt good not to be alone. He followed closely behind the boys. Outside, they took up most of the sidewalk.

"You got a lot to learn, man," Felix said to Angelo.

"Yeah," Darius agreed. "Like stop walking like you're a *turista*!" Darius angled his head up and walked funny, looking at everything. "Wow, look! What's a Pizza Pizza?" Angelo could see Darius was mocking him.

As the boys laughed, Felix said, "You got to walk around like you own the place."

Angelo nodded.

"I'll show you." Felix turned sharply onto

the road, cutting in front of a cab. The driver honked his horn and Felix gave him the finger.

Darius howled. "That's how you do it!"

Marcus said, "He's right. You might see people that look like you. But you ain't in Manila no more."

Darius added, "Bring some fried pig head to lunch and you'll see!"

They all laughed, including Angelo.

Chapter 4

Pulong (Meeting)

Angelo followed Felix, Darius, and Marcus to a gas station, past some cars filling up. He was confused why they were there. Felix took the lead, entering the store attached to the station.

The first thing Angelo noticed was the look the boys got from the guy at the counter. He didn't look happy to see them. Darius broke from the group and walked up to the counter. That's when Angelo felt a tug. It was Marcus pulling him toward Felix.

They strolled down an aisle and stopped at the back, by the wall of fridges. Cold air escaped as Felix opened the door. Angelo watched as Marcus pulled energy drinks from the fridge and placed them in the pockets of Felix's baggy jeans.

Marcus said to Angelo, "Try not to stare."

So Angelo looked away. He was kind of in shock as he looked at the ceiling. At the floor. At the items on the shelves. He glanced to the front of the store. Darius was trying to convince the man to sell him a pack of cigarettes. Angelo could see that the man behind the counter was getting mad at Darius. Taking a quick look toward the back of the store, Darius left the counter and joined the boys.

Felix closed the fridge. He turned to Darius as he came down the aisle. "What's up?"

Darius spoke loudly. "This fool doesn't believe I'm nineteen."

"What?" Felix said, seeming surprised. "Well, forget him. Let's get out of here."

Angelo was the last out of the shop. He followed the boys as they walked around the back of the gas station. They all stopped on a side street.

Felix dug into his pockets and pulled out the energy drinks. "You cool?" he asked Angelo.

Angelo tried not to show how he was really feeling. He was ashamed that he hadn't just walked away. He'd never stolen anything in his life. *Why*, he wondered, *am I still here?*

Then Felix tossed him a drink. Angelo stared at it for a moment.

Darius stepped towards Angelo. "What, you're too good to drink it?" he said with a frown.

Angelo cracked open the can and drank. As the cold liquid flowed down his throat, he tried not to think about what his grandfather Paolo would say.

***

It took a moment for Angelo to get his bearings. He had been dreaming of home again. Of being on Paolo's fishing boat. Angelo opened his eyes and saw that he was on the pullout futon. He got up, feeling sad, and moved to the kitchen. His mom was long gone to work. There was a new note waiting for him. Over a glass of water, he took a peek.

You are not alone. I am here for you. Eat breakfast.

***

"Angelo." At school, Angelo was walking down the hall when he heard his name.

It was a teacher. "We talked on your first day here," said the man. "It was a busy one for you. I understand if you don't remember me."

Angelo didn't. Too much was new for him to remember anything.

"I'm Mr. Williams. I'm the guidance counsellor. My job is to help you transition." Mr. Williams was Black and his head was shaved. He wore jeans and a blazer with a yellow tie. "Step into my office for a moment."

Mr. Williams offered Angelo a chair before he sat behind his desk. "How are you doing?"

Angelo shrugged. It wasn't much, but it was the truth. He didn't know how he was doing.

"I understand," said Mr. Williams. "You're in a tough position. But you need to start seeing the good side. I know you're going to say, 'whatever.' But if you study hard, get a better grasp on English, your education can take you anywhere."

Angelo didn't say whatever. He didn't say anything.

"Not ready to talk." Mr. Williams leaned back in his chair. "I get it."

The two of them sat in awkward silence for a bit. Angelo wanted out of the room. It was clear Mr. Williams wanted into Angelo's thoughts.

Mr. Williams broke the silence. "Seeing students succeed is my favourite part of my job. Sometimes that takes a while. But know that I am here for you." Angelo's left foot twitched. His hand-me-down boots were beat up and covered in salt stains.

"Do you have anything to say to me at this point? No judgment."

Angelo shook his head.

"Well, if you'd like to leave my office, you need to say something. A start."

Angelo muttered, "I'll do my homework."

Mr. Williams leaned, pressing his right ear forward. "He talks!" Then he clapped his hands and rubbed them together. "Okay, that's good to hear. Your teachers will be happy."

"I can go?"

Mr. Williams nodded. Angelo stood up and went to the door. As he turned the knob, Mr. Williams said, "One more thing."

Angelo stopped and turned.

"I need to hear a 'What, Mr. Williams?'"

"What, Mr. Williams?"

"Please think hard about choosing the right friends. And smile."

Angelo left.

Chapter 5

Katotohanan (Reality)

After school, Angelo walked across the back field of the school to meet up with the boys. Felix had asked him to come.

He thought about what Mr. Williams had hinted at about the boys. Did Angelo really care what Williams thought? Did he have any other offers of friendship? The answer was a big no to both of them.

Angelo said, "*Kamusta*," asking the boys how they were. The boys waved him over.

Angelo followed Felix, Marcus, and Darius onto a streetcar.

They got seats in the back. Angelo mostly listened as they laughed and made jokes about people they passed on the sidewalk. He looked out the windows as the long streetcar snaked its way west along the busy street. One stop past Yonge Street, Felix led the way out. They walked for a bit until Felix held up his hand. Angelo stopped, becoming suspicious. What were they doing in this part of the city?

"This is it," Felix announced, "your education starts now."

"Yeah," Marcus added, "time to open your eyes."

Angelo replied slowly, "Okay."

"What do you see?" Felix asked.

"Busy street. Lots of people."

"You're looking at money! People walking around in expensive clothes, going on expensive vacations. They work in these nice buildings. What's in these buildings?"

Angelo looked up. He saw tall glass and cement buildings.

"Banks! Money!" Felix was getting worked up. "Bankers, lawyers. Reality check. We live in poverty. And these people live in the fancy homes that our moms clean. They have kids that our moms look after when they get home from private school."

"That's how things work when you're Filipino!" Darius yelled out angrily at a man rushing by.

Marcus pulled on Angelo's shoulder. "Look around, man. We don't get no respect. These people don't care about us."

Angelo nodded. He remembered Yvonne wanting to show him around when he first arrived. But he was jet-lagged and in a terrible mood on that first day in Canada. So things didn't go as Yvonne had planned. He knew she had hopes of him running off the plane and into her arms, like the excited little boy she had left behind. Nope. That day, Yvonne showed him a few Toronto landmarks, but he didn't pay much attention. He wouldn't be able to tell the hockey arena from the baseball stadium.

On the busy sidewalk, Angelo felt just as much an outsider as he had that first day. Everyone else had somewhere to go. Angelo felt like he didn't matter. He was slowly realizing that if he vanished, no one's life would really be affected.

In the Philippines, Angelo and his grandfather caught fish and sold it in the village. People relied on him. They would call out compliments and thank-yous if he and Paolo caught a really big haul of fish.

Angelo was pulled back into reality when Felix tapped his arm.

"What do you think? Who's it going to be?"

Darius pointed. "Across the street, right of the bus stop. In the long, black coat."

Felix nodded. "Looks like he's on an important phone call. Let's strike while it's hot. Darius, you got this?"

Darius nodded. "Yeah."

The group broke up. Marcus stayed on lookout while Darius continued up the street. Angelo followed Felix as he jaywalked in front of a honking taxi. Felix extended his middle finger at the taxi.

"Look at that guy," Felix said, nodding to the man in the black coat. "He thinks we're going to take his wallet."

Angelo looked at the target. "We're not. Right?"

Felix didn't respond.

To Angelo, it felt like he was in a movie. He could hear the music building suspense as he stood, caught in a stare-down with the man in the black coat.

Felix sputtered with laughter. "Acting all cool and calm. But underneath, his mind is racing." His voice changed, his Tagalog accent coming out more. Angelo listened to the shorter vowel sounds and softer *t*'s and *d*'s. "He's thinking, 'Who are these punks? Probably high on drugs and looking to get their next fix. This is what's wrong with our country. Youth ain't got no direction.'"

Angelo held in his laughter and shoved his hands deeper in his pockets to keep warm. He was starting to rethink what Mr. Williams had told him. Stealing energy drinks was one thing. But whatever was about to go down now seemed a whole lot worse. Plus, it was outside on a busy street with lots of witnesses. As they got closer, Angelo wondered what the plan was. Tackle the man? Knock him down and take his stuff?

The man tugged at his coat and grasped his suitcase on wheels in a tighter grip.

Yeah, Angelo thought, *the man is definitely scared.*

Then suddenly, Darius appeared from behind the man. He was coming in from the other direction. That was when Felix led Angelo into a sharp ninety-degree turn away from the man.

Over his shoulder, Angelo spotted Darius pulling off a briefcase that was sitting on top of the suitcase. Angelo quickly turned away. He and Felix were the distraction. Darius was the one making the grab.

When they were across the street back to where they started, Felix said with a smile, "And that's how it's done."

Angelo nodded. "What if someone saw?"

"You'd know."

"What do you mean?"

Felix answered, "If someone saw, we'd be running right now. But no one saw we were in on it. So we walk to our meeting place, pretending that we're lost. Why else would two Filipino kids be walking down a street paved in gold?"

The boys passed a parking garage and turned down an alley. It was clean — no garbage and no graffiti. Angelo saw Marcus and Darius waiting for them. Darius handed the briefcase over to Felix.

"Good job, boys. Let's make this part quick before Whitey knows it's missing." Felix pulled a screwdriver from his jacket and dug it deep into the leather around the opening of the briefcase.

The boys formed a circle cover around him.

A couple more tries, and the leather started to rip and peel back. Felix drove the screwdriver deeper, twisting and turning it. Finally, the case popped open.

Felix stepped back to reveal the contents. He pulled out a gold pen, a metal business card case, and a leather notebook. When he uncovered a wafer-thin laptop in a fabric sleeve, Felix said, "Here we are."

Marcus pulled out a white, plastic grocery bag and unfolded it. Felix filled it with his new belongings. "Let's get out of here," he said, as he dumped the briefcase onto the ground.

Back on the streetcar, the boys celebrated.

Marcus complimented Angelo. "You did great. Kept your cool and didn't blow it."

Angelo smiled sheepishly.

"Yeah, man," Darius started, "you're just one of the *lalaki*."

"That's right," Felix repeated, "one of the boys. We've pulled in a good haul today."

"Leave it all to Felix," Darius said. "He can sell anything. And get a good price for it."

As the streetcar made its way through the busy downtown traffic, Marcus and Darius continued to rag Angelo. They messed with his hair and swore in Tagalog.

Angelo played along, bonding with his new friends. He knew that among all the people crowded on the streetcar, no one had any idea what was in the plastic shopping bag.

Chapter 6

Ang Reyna
(The Queen)

The subway screeched in a dark tunnel. Angelo's eyes picked out all the cell phones that were lit up in people's hands.

Yvonne leaned in. "You need to keep your voice down when we get there. Any questions, just ask me," she said.

He nodded.

"And if she asks you anything, you respond with, 'Yes, Mrs. Harrington.'"

The train broke through the underground

and light poured in. The train stopped and exchanged people getting off for those getting on. Marcus had explained the PA day to Angelo. Students were off for the day while teachers got time to meet and talk about them. That was bad news for Angelo. Yvonne had been called by Mr. Williams about Angelo's incomplete homework. Angelo just wanted to stay home, but Yvonne didn't want him watching TV all day.

As they walked off the subway and got onto a bus, Yvonne laid down more demands. "Mrs. Harrington is very picky about her house. So don't touch anything. Hang your coat up and take your shoes off when we enter."

This lady sounds like a nasty queen, Angelo thought. Five stops later, he followed Yvonne off the bus. He was surprised at how far she had to travel each day to get to work.

The sidewalk was empty except for a man walking a dog. Angelo smirked. The dog was wearing a colourful sweater and matching boots. The dog was dressed for the weather better than Angelo.

Continuing down the street, Angelo took in the houses nestled between large trees without leaves. He tried to guess how many apartments the size of theirs could fit into one of these houses. Driveway after driveway, each monster home looked bigger than the last. It reminded him of the mansions he once saw in Forbes Park in Manila.

Yvonne finally turned them onto a driveway that made a half-circle in front of a house. Angelo looked around in awe. The house was one storey, but it sprawled to take up as much space as a city block. It had too many windows to count in one look. A shiny black BMW SUV with tinted windows was parked near the large double front doors.

"Not there," Yvonne said as Angelo headed for that entrance. She guided Angelo to a second door along the side of the house by the garage. "The maid's door." She punched a code into a keypad and the door unlocked.

Angelo noticed that the passcode was his birthday month and day.

Yvonne saw that Angelo had picked up on her code. "Everything I've ever done," Yvonne said, "has been for you."

"You lived here?"

"While I was Jacob's nanny. He grew up. So I became the housekeeper and moved out." She brushed her feet on the outside mat. She patted Angelo gently on the cheek. "Now don't say or do anything."

The door swung open and Angelo stepped into a new world. The house had vaulted ceilings and reflective marble floors. The furniture looked like it belonged in a museum. The whole place echoed of money and good taste. Angelo could see why Yvonne had told him not to touch anything.

Once his shoes were off, he was led down a long hallway that opened into a kitchen as big as in a restaurant. As fancy as the kitchen was, the thing Angelo really noticed was the view through the windows. A large wooden deck led out to a huge back yard with a pool that was covered for winter.

What a waste, he thought, *to have a pool and not be able to use it for so much of the year.*

Yvonne got his attention. "Now, your job is to sit here and do your homework while I work."

Angelo pulled some homework from his backpack, even though he had no intention of doing it. He'd spend the day thinking about what it would be like to live in a place like this.

"I have to get started," Yvonne said. "Any questions, Angelo?"

He looked up at her and saw she already had a blue apron wrapped around her clothes. She held a bucket full of cleaning supplies in her hand. "Get started now," she urged.

Angelo bent his head, seeming to do what he was told. Suddenly, the sound of a woman talking caught his attention. She made a big entrance into the kitchen, wearing a fur-lined jacket and carrying an armload of shopping bags. She took off her jacket to reveal a sharp looking suit. Angelo could see she was all blinged up with sparkling jewellery. *The Queen has arrived*, Angelo thought.

She was speaking quickly and he couldn't quite pick out the words. Finally, she noticed Angelo and Yvonne. She held up her index finger at them, showing off a long, manicured fingernail. It signalled that they should wait.

Angelo and Yvonne froze as she took her time to end the string of orders she was making into the phone.

The Queen removed her sunglasses and stepped toward Angelo. She lowered her finger and used it to beckon him to her. Her bracelets made a clanging sound. "Well, there he is! Welcome to Canada, young man."

Angelo offered a half-smirk. He noticed her face was very tanned. *Which of us looks more like we've come from somewhere warm?* he wondered.

"Now don't be so shy," she went on. "Your

darling mother has been waiting forever for you to arrive."

Yvonne laughed nervously. "He is a very shy boy, Mrs. Harrington."

The Queen pursed her lips together. "Well, I suppose it takes time to adjust. Now, Yvonne, put some food out for the poor boy."

She smiled at Angelo. But he didn't see any sympathy for him in that smile.

"Tell me, Yvonne, how are things going at the Millers' house?" The Queen didn't wait for Yvonne to answer. Instead, she said to Angelo, "I got many of my good friends to hire your mother as a housekeeper after she moved out."

Angelo nodded.

"Things are good, Mrs. Harrington. The Millers are nice," replied Yvonne.

"Good to hear. A couple of reminders. My son Jacob and his friends have made a mess of the rec room. And we're having an important party this evening. So please make sure the living room is sparkling."

"Yes, Mrs. Harrington."

"Oh, we are going to be skiing on the long weekend at Blue Mountain. Will you be able to work on the holiday Monday? I'll make it up to you some time later."

"Yes, Mrs. Harrington."

The Queen left and Angelo let out a long, loud burst of air. He had never seen anyone so bossy.

Yvonne said, "Don't be rude." She pulled a plate of sandwiches and a glass of juice from the fridge. She placed them on the table next to Angelo and said, "Stay here."

"What if I have to use the washroom?"

"Down that hallway. Second door on the right."

Chapter 7

Tukso
(Temptation)

Alone in the kitchen, Angelo looked at his work. He decided to reach for a sandwich first, not caring that he had just eaten breakfast. He took one bite and was surprised at how tasty it was. He took another sandwich into his open hand, double-fisting them. Then he stood up and moved to the doors leading out to the back yard. The snow was cleaner and whiter than it was where they lived. Standing in the warm kitchen, Angelo could see how winter was almost pretty. *I was born into the wrong family*, he thought. He tried to picture how amazing it would be in the summer. The warm sun and the blue water from the pool would make it almost like home.

He finished his sandwich in one big bite. He was about to start on the second when he was startled by two boys entering the kitchen.

Angelo could see they were a few years younger than he was. They stopped talking to each other to look at him.

Angelo looked at them, sandwich in hand. He felt like he was a thief. He slowly lowered his hands to try to hide the food. But it was too late.

One boy asked, "Who the hell are you?" He turned to the other boy.

Angelo didn't know what to say. Besides, his mouth was full.

Then the other said, "Oh yeah, he's our maid's kid."

The first boy shrugged. "Jacob, why is he

eating all your food?"

Angelo looked at Jacob. He was the Queen's son. Angelo had heard about him and always wondered what he looked like.

"Nah, that stuff's old," Jacob said with a grimace. He pulled drinks out of the fridge and grabbed a bag of chips, leaving the cupboard door open. The boys started stuffing their faces with chips. It was like Angelo wasn't even there.

"Oh, I have to show you what I just got for my birthday," said Jacob. "You're going to freak!"

The boys left the kitchen.

Angelo looked down at his sandwich. He wondered how something "old" could taste so good. He placed it back on the plate and drank all the juice in his cup. He noticed that the boys had left a total mess of chip crumbs and spills on the counter. A mess that Yvonne would have to clean up.

Angelo rocked back and forth in the kitchen chair. He thought about the two boys. He wondered what they were doing. Then he wondered what kind of job someone would need to have to afford a house like this.

Angelo decided that he would find the bathroom. He didn't have to go, but he wanted to see what it was like. He followed Yvonne's directions and moved down the hallway, sliding a little on the shiny floor in his socks.

Family pictures lined the route. Some were of vacations under palm trees and over ski hills. Most were of Jacob. Seeing the boy at stages from babyhood to the kid he saw in the kitchen, Angelo was reminded of all the years Yvonne spent here. While he was living in the Philippines without a mother, Jacob had his own mom plus Angelo's to take care of him.

The idea angered Angelo so much he had to resist the urge to punch the photos of little Jacob. And then Angelo stopped at one picture of the boy in front of a birthday cake shaped like a train. There were five big candles on the fancy cake and the little boy was smiling at the camera. In the background, Angelo could see a woman smiling fondly at five-year-old Jacob. It was Yvonne.

If Angelo had cared enough, he'd have let out a tear. Instead, he bottled in what he was feeling — the sadness and resentment. Suddenly, this house didn't hold the same level of awe or wonder for him. This was where Yvonne had decided to spend her years as a mother. As a mother to the wrong kid. This was what she'd left Angelo for.

All Angelo wanted was out. As he stepped toward the bathroom, an open door caught his eye. Angelo took a few steps down the hall and stood close to the entrance of a bedroom. He could hear Jacob talking to his friend. A step closer and he was close enough to peer inside.

The large room had framed movie posters. The desk boasted a huge computer monitor with big speakers and a gaming controller. Next to the bed was an electric guitar with amplifier. But as nice as the room was, as full as it was of pricey stuff, it was equally a total mess. The bed wasn't made and clothes littered the floor. A big part of Angelo felt bad that it was Yvonne who had to clean up the mess. He hoped she was being paid enough to put up with this kind of work. But based on the size and location of their apartment, he knew the answer was a big no.

Jacob was showing off his latest belonging.

"You got a signed Wayne Gretzky rookie card?" Jacob's friend was clearly excited.

"Yes," Jacob nodded, "for my birthday." He held out the coloured piece of cardboard, protected by a clear wrapping.

"It's a collectible, Jacob. You know how much that's worth?"

"A lot," Jacob said. "But I'm not selling it. Gretzky is my hero." He placed the card on his desk. "Let's get out of here."

Angelo scurried backward into the bathroom. He closed the door as he heard the boys walk by. Then he waited a few moments before stepping back into the hall. He stood in front of Jacob's bedroom. He ignored the voice inside his head telling him, *No, don't go in there! What, are you crazy?* Instead, he took a step inside the messy room.

The images from the wall in the hall spun around like in a whirl of bitterness in Angelo's head. He thought of all the time Yvonne had spent in here in this house. Jacob had something that was important to Angelo . . . Angelo's mom. Angelo bit down on his bottom lip to fight back the tears. Then he decided to take something important from Jacob. He slid the hockey card into his pocket and walked out.

✳ ✳ ✳

Angelo strolled down Parliament Street. He had both hands in his pockets and a grin on his face. He pulled on a door that caused a chime to ring. The restaurant was empty except for a sprinkling of diners and an elderly woman at the counter. They all turned to look at him.

Angelo stepped to the counter and pulled his hands out of his pockets. In one hand was a small stack of rolled bills that Felix had given him for his "work." Angelo looked at the lit-up menu and pointed. "*Pansit*," he said, placing his order.

The woman nodded and told him it was eight dollars.

A few moments later, a bowl of noodles and vegetables arrived. It wasn't exactly like home. But it tasted great and warmed his insides. He took another spoonful and dreaded having to go to back to the apartment. Back to the Filipino Centre. Back to the life Yvonne wanted for him.

Chapter 8

Patunayan
(Prove)

At school the next day, Felix and the boys were excited for Angelo. When Felix saw him, he said, "Today it's your turn, Angelo. You have to show us what you've got."

"That's right," Darius said. "The free ride is over. You have to start delivering."

Angelo nodded.

A cute girl caught Felix's attention and he followed her, laying down some moves. Darius turned and urged him to go get her.

Angelo took the chance to ask Marcus for help. "I don't really know what I'm doing. What if I get caught?"

"You won't, because you got us."

"So what do I do?"

"You look for the right person at the right moment. It's all about distraction."

Marcus pointed at a student by his locker. "Take a look over there. You don't need a distraction because he's working on his lock combo. It's a perfect time to take something."

Angelo couldn't believe they were talking about stealing at school.

Marcus continued, "You walk by and bump into him. He's so annoyed by the bump, all you do is take what he has."

"That easy?"

"Want me to show you?"

"Here? Now? Sure."

Marcus walked to the end of the hallway, then turned around. He passed a long row of lockers, looking for a new target. A girl was checking herself out in a small mirror inside her locker door. Marcus turned like he was distracted by something and ran into the girl.

As she turned and screamed out, "Watch it!" Marcus moved to her other side. He reached down with his left hand and scooped a book from her backpack.

He said, "I'm so sorry." At the same time, he tucked the book in his left armpit.

She said, "Better be," before returning to her mirror.

Marcus sauntered toward Angelo with a big smile on his face. "Here." He put the book in Angelo's hand.

"That was so smooth," Angelo said. He didn't know what to do with the book, though.

Marcus said, "Thanks," and took back the book. "Once you got what you want, get out of there." He flicked the book onto the ground. It skidded like a stone on water before crashing into a garbage can.

"I can't do that."

"Yes you can. The more of us working together, the easier it'll be. It's kind of like basketball. We're a team. Some on offence, some on defence. Play your position well and we all win."

"Stealing is like basketball? Weird, but I get it," Angelo said.

Angelo wondered what his brother would think about him learning how to steal. *It's kind of like the saying, hangga't makitid ang kumot, matutong mamaluktot,* he thought. While the blanket is short, learn how to bend. He thought back to many of his friends who had paid the teacher for good grades. It's not like corruption and stealing didn't exist in the Philippines.

"You know what I mean," Marcus said. "It's a huge thrill knowing you can get almost anything you want. People here have so much stuff and money, they don't even miss it. Or we just give them a chance to go shopping for something new and better to replace the lost things."

The bell rang and teachers started breaking up crowds to get students into classrooms. Angelo thanked Marcus and headed to his first period class. But he still wasn't sure if he'd be able to steal anything.

* * *

The boys walked in a pack across Dundas Square. Darius asked Felix, "So you make out with the girl?"

"Her name's Tracey," Felix responded. "I'm working on doing a whole lot more."

The boys howled.

Marcus said, "Good answer," and high-fived Felix.

They passed a guy playing the guitar and asking for money. Angelo wondered why someone would do that in cold weather. He didn't look like he was making much money at it. Across the street, he could see the Eaton Centre. This was where he had to prove himself.

All day at school, he'd thought of excuses to get out of it. Then he realized that he didn't want out. These guys were all he had.

Across the sidewalk, Darius made fun of a man spouting words about God into a loudspeaker. Angelo just went around the sidewalk preacher. In the Philippines, Angelo went to church a lot. Paolo would make him pray for Yvonne, that she would be safe halfway around the world. And that one day, she would come home. Except that "one day" never happened.

Being inside the Eaton Centre reminded Angelo of being at the SM Mega Mall in Manila. He'd go there with his brother at the end of a school term to shop. It had been his reward for getting good grades.

The boys stood against a railing overlooking a huge drop. Angelo was impressed by the three floors of stores and the massive glass ceiling arching above. People were swarming and buzzing all around. He imagined himself coming here with his hard-earned money and walking into a store to do some shopping.

The first thing he'd do is get some new clothes. Then he could trash the used clothes Yvonne had scrounged for him. Second thing would be a phone. He'd always wanted a really nice phone.

"This place is yours," Felix said. "Take the lead and we will follow."

Angelo hesitated. He didn't know his way around, so he couldn't direct the boys. He rode the escalator down a level, taking the moment of standing to think. *This is just like school*, he thought. *Find someone who's not looking and make your move.*

Angelo stepped off the escalator with an idea. He'd skip a step and just steal a phone he could keep as his own. He walked with the same confidence as the guys around him. "So, Felix, are you guys gonna run the distraction?" he asked.

"Whatever you want, man."

Marcus said, "Pick a target."

Angelo eyed the people going by. He felt powerful, knowing that all he had to do was pick someone. Maybe it was the type of stores on this level, but he just wasn't feeling it.

He led them to the end of the floor and down another escalator. The escalator gave him more time to think. *Don't make this personal,* he said to himself. *Just find someone and do it.*

Along the main floor, Darius stepped in. "He's not ready. Maybe this just isn't his —"

Marcus jumped in. "Give him time. It's okay to be a little nervous."

"Nervous gets you taken down."

Felix held up his hand. "Stop it." He turned to Angelo. "It's this floor or no floor."

Angelo nodded. He kept looking for a chance, a sign. And he found it. In the middle of the lower level was a huge fountain. The spot screamed distraction. On one side was a set of escalators, and on the other, glass elevators. In the middle, the fountain spat water two floors up into the air.

All kinds of people sat around the fountain. Angelo circled it and quickly found his target. A man in a brown leather jacket and black knitted cap was on his phone. His work bag rested under his right leg.

Angelo whispered to Marcus, "When I signal you, make some noise."

Felix said, "Whatever happens, meet me in the men's room over there. We take what we can and dump the rest."

Felix left. Marcus nodded at Angelo. "Okay. You call it."

Chapter 9

Nahuli (Caught)

Angelo sat next to the man with the bag. His back was to the fountain. To the right, a woman in a hijab had a baby in a stroller in front of her.

Around him, the world slowed down. He took a peek at the bag from the corner of his eyes. It was black and it had a handle. The baby next to him made a loud sound and almost everyone turned toward it. Toward him.

This baby's making it harder for me, Angelo

thought. It was now or never. Angelo made eye contact with Marcus and nodded his head.

Marcus responded by turning to Darius and screaming, "Why'd you do that!"

"Do what?" Darius screamed back.

Marcus gave Darius a shove and shouted, "You know what!"

Angelo had a moment while everyone was looking at the boys. He reached down and lifted the work bag. Then he stood and stepped away. He held the bag close to his chest, like he was running with a football. Behind him, he could hear the boys still going at it.

I have it! Angelo thought. *I pulled it off!* He ran up the escalator, then curled toward the bank of elevators. And then he heard it: "My bag! He took my bag!"

Panic kicked in. Angelo started to speed walk. People were eyeing him as the man's voice screamed out, "Stop him!"

Angelo had to think fast. How was he going to get to the men's washroom and meet up with the boys? Then he spotted a security guard. He knew that getting to Felix wasn't going to happen. He needed to get out of the mall.

Angelo heard the ding of an elevator arriving. He elbowed through the waiting crowd to get in it just as the doors closed. He pressed against the elevator window as it started to rise. He looked down at the fountain as it shot up a stream of water. Angelo felt a little better.

The elevator arrived at the next floor and the doors opened. Angelo made a split-second decision to exit. He clutched the bag and slowed his walk to normal so he wouldn't stick out.

Angelo wasn't out of the mess or the mall yet. He heard the man again, his voice coming from somewhere closer than he liked. "My bag!"

Angelo decided to turn a sharp corner. He reached into the bag to get what he could out of it.

"Stop him!" he heard again.

He kept moving.

As much as he wanted his first job to go well, he had no choice but to ditch the bag. He tossed the bag between a banking machine and a garbage can. Up ahead, he saw the mall doors. A part of him wondered if he should make a run for it.

With the mall doors in sight, Angelo felt a firm hand on his shoulder. He turned to see a security guard.

"You're coming with me, punk."

Angelo felt a wave of sickness crashing in his stomach. He was taken to the mall security office located down a long hall between two stores. He was ushered into a small room with a desk and some chairs. He was placed in one of those chairs.

The security guard who brought him in wore a white shirt, dark pants, and a utility belt. He stood above Angelo. "I'm Dave with mall security. You've been detained for attempting to steal someone else's property."

Heart racing, Angelo kept his eyes down.

Dave had a pen and clipboard. "What's your name?"

Angelo didn't respond.

He tapped the pen on the clipboard. "Do you have any sharp objects on you?"

Angelo sat on his hands to try to control his nerves. He shook his head.

Dave's voice grew louder. "I need a yes or a no."

Angelo's voice cracked. "No."

"Drugs?"

Angelo said no a little louder. His mind raced to Yvonne. She'd be so mad. She'd come down hard on him when she found out. He could see her all out of breath and deeply disappointed. She would clutch her purse and say something like: "I bring you to this new country and you repay me by breaking the law!"

The phone in the room rang loudly and Dave answered it. There was a lot of "Oh yeah?" and "Really?" before he hung up. He turned to Angelo and put down his clipboard, replacing it in his hand with a small, white Styrofoam cup. He took a careful sip before asking, "Who are you here with?"

The boys, Angelo thought. *Did any of them get caught?*

His first attempt and he got caught. What a disaster. They'd probably disown him for bringing attention to them. And if any of them got caught — they'd definitely disown him. Angelo pictured Felix sitting in a room like this one.

Dave repeated himself. "Who are you here with? Who was with you?"

Angelo muttered, "No one."

"That's a lie!" Dave screamed. "Where are your friends?"

Angelo recoiled into his seat.

"You're going to make this a whole lot harder on yourself than it has to be if you won't talk."

Isn't it obvious? Angelo thought. *I took the bag.* He didn't know what to say.

He looked up when the door opened. He half expected to see Yvonne. But it was a female security guard. She wore the same uniform as Dave and had her light brown hair pulled back tightly into a ponytail. "Got anything, Dave?" she asked.

Dave said, "No."

"Well, I have the man out here. Found the bag on the floor by the wall."

"Anything missing?"

"Just checking on that." The woman turned to Angelo. "You should co-operate. You'll get nowhere fast by lying to us." Then she left the room.

"Yeah," Dave said, holding the clipboard again. "You're not the first person your age to sit in this seat. If you want us to help you in any way, you need to talk to us." He paused. "Do you speak English? Can you understand me?"

Angelo didn't say anything. He hid under a shell of denial.

"Okay. Be that way." Dave left and closed the door behind him.

Angelo looked up. All kinds of feelings swirled around in his mind, shame, fear, anger. He wondered what life would be like with a criminal record.

The door reopened and both security guards entered.

Dave started, "I thought we should call the cops. Let them deal with you."

"But lucky for you, nothing is missing or damaged," the woman added. "The man you tried to steal from is not pressing charges."

Angelo was confused.

The woman opened the door. "Get out of here. But if you ever come by this mall again, we'll be watching for you."

Chapter 10

Libre (Free)

Angelo moved quickly through the security area. It wasn't until he was back in the busy mall that he realized he truly was free. First thing was to find the boys. There was no sign of anyone in the men's room where they had agreed to meet. It was strange for Angelo to go back to the fountain where everything started. Again, no sign of the boys.

Out of the mall, Angelo passed the street corner preacher. He checked right and left, then decided to bail. On a streetcar heading home, he replayed in his mind the moment he grabbed the bag. After everything Marcus had shown him, what had he done wrong? His target was on the phone and then had looked up at Marcus and Darius — the perfect distraction.

Angelo thought that he should have moved behind the fountain to give himself more cover. Also, he should have taken the bag the exact moment the boys took attention away from Angelo. Waiting even those split seconds had cost him escape time.

The streetcar stopped at Parliament Street and Angelo got off. It was already dark out. He knew that Yvonne would be mad. But her level of mad wouldn't be as bad as those security guards.

He entered their building and rode the elevator up. Most people were coming home from work. Angelo opened the front door and found Yvonne at the kitchen counter. Her arms were crossed, her face stern.

"Really, Angelo?" she said. "This is the respect I get?"

Angelo blew past her and flopped down on the couch. The woman who shared the apartment went into her bedroom and closed the door.

Yvonne followed Angelo to the couch. "You have nothing to say?"

Two grillings in one day, Angelo thought.

"Angelo, please talk to me."

Angelo remained quiet.

Yvonne uncrossed her arms. "In the future, please be home on time."

Angelo reached for the remote and turned on the TV. He was not looking forward to school the next day.

✸✸✸

But the next day came much too quickly. Getting up was hard for Angelo. And then it took him a few tries to build the courage to enter the school.

"Angelo!" Marcus was the first to find him. "You okay?"

"No. I got caught."

"What? All I saw was you taking off. Then the guy yelled after you, but you were gone. We couldn't find you."

"They found me. The guards. They took me to a room and yelled at me. They threatened to call the police. I thought I was going to jail."

"They arrested you!"

Felix and Darius walked up together.

"There he is," Felix said. "The felon."

"Yeah," Darius added. "You going to do hard time or what?"

"They didn't arrest me," Angelo replied. "They let me go with a big warning. And said they'd be looking for me next time I went to that mall."

"Stupid mall security. They think they're the cops, but they're nothing. Nothing to worry about. We're going back there whenever we want," Darius said.

Angelo nodded. "They get any of you?"

"No. So the big question," Felix started. "What did you tell them?"

"Nothing. I kept quiet even though they pushed."

Felix grabbed Angelo by the neck and pulled him in close. "Be honest. Did you confess?"

"No. I said nothing." Angelo felt Felix's fingers jabbing into the skin of the back of his neck. He felt the warmth of Felix's breath on his face.

Felix held him for a few seconds and then finally let go. Angelo thought he was trying to read his mind. "You still need to deliver something," Felix told him. "You've got to the end of first period. And I want something I can make a profit on."

The boys followed Felix away, so Angelo was left alone as he entered his first period class. His mind was racing as he barely heard the anthem and announcements. He scanned the classroom for possible targets. Pencils and binders would be worthless. He needed a big-ticket item. And in this classroom, the only thing to come to mind was a cell phone.

He could make out the imprint of cell phones in pockets. Some girls had theirs half sticking out the back pocket of their jeans. Sliding a phone from there would be very dangerous. Marcus's advice ran through Angelo's head. He saw a girl in front of him sneak a peek at her phone behind her textbook. Angelo had found his target.

Next, he knew he'd have to create a distraction. The math teacher started presenting the day's lesson on the chalkboard. Most students didn't listen or bother to even look at what the teacher was doing until he turned around and asked the class a question.

Angelo knew that this was his now-or-never moment. He took a big breath, grabbed his pencil, and headed for the pencil sharpener. He passed too close to the desk next to him and knocked over a water bottle. It got the attention of a few people around him, including the girl with the cell phone.

Angelo stepped close to the girl's desk. It looked like he was moving away from the spilled water. He lifted the girl's textbook enough to slide out her cell phone. He palmed it tightly and brought it to his side, then slid it into his pocket. Angelo moved to the sink to grab paper towel. He turned to help clean up the spill as some people snickered.

"Just hurry and wipe it up," the teacher ordered.

Angelo cleared the mess and returned to his seat. He slid the cell phone out of his pocket and used his textbook to cover it. He pressed hard on the power button until it went black. Then he sat at his desk and refocused on the math lesson. He tried his best to contain his excitement while the girl tried to figure out what had happened to her cell phone without drawing the teacher's attention.

The bell rang and Angelo was quick to get out. He found Felix and the boys in the washroom.

"What you got?" Felix asked.

Angelo removed the phone from his pocket. Marcus was first to congratulate him with a pat on the shoulder.

Felix turned on the phone, nodded, and offered a half-smile.

Angelo went to follow the boys out of the washroom, but they suddenly stopped. Angelo was still behind the door when he heard Mr. Williams's voice.

"Any of you boys see Angelo?"

Angelo stepped deeper into the washroom.

"No," Marcus said. "Haven't seen him around today."

Angelo smiled as the boys covered for him, and Mr. Williams left.

Chapter 11

Kumpisal (Confession)

Angelo neared their apartment building. He did a double take at the entrance when he saw Yvonne standing in front of the doors. That scared Angelo. He tried to move past her into the building, but she grabbed his arm and stopped him.

"Ouch."

She held her grip.

"Stop that." Angelo tried to wiggle free. But her grip was tight on his arm under his thick jacket.

"I said I was sorry for being late yesterday," he said. He thought about yelling for help, but didn't want to look stupid.

Yvonne's face tightened like she was fighting back tears. *"Kapag hindi ka umuwi sa oras nang uwian hindi kita papaloobin sa bahay."*

"I thought you wanted me to only speak English?"

Yvonne repeated slowly, this time in English. "If you don't come home on time, I won't let you in the house."

For a moment Angelo couldn't figure out if she was upset or sad. If it was both, he knew he was a dead man.

"I hope you didn't do it," Yvonne said.

Angelo tried to shrug, but it was hard with his arm in her iron grip. "I'm on time. Ready to go to the centre to do my homework."

"Not that," Yvonne spat out.

Angelo pulled his arm free and took a step backward to safety. He couldn't figure out what had gotten into her. Why was she so furious?

"I got a call —"

Then it hit him. Angelo thought back to the Eaton Centre and his time in mall security. *Did they find out my name?* Angelo wondered. *Did they call the police?*

"If you did it, then come clean. Right here and right now."

Angelo began to overheat. Panic attacked. But he couldn't figure out how this could happen. *I told them nothing,* he reminded himself. He looked up at Yvonne, helpless.

She stepped outside.

Angelo paused.

"Come on, now," Yvonne said.

It took a second for Angelo to register that she wanted him to follow her. Out on the street, Angelo had a hard time keeping up. Yvonne speed walked along the sidewalk.

"Where we going?" Angelo asked.

Yvonne didn't answer. The first surprise for Angelo was when they turned west. Angelo's mind filled with dark thoughts. West would take them to the Eaton Centre. She was going to take him there and feed him to mall security.

Yvonne offered a "keep up" before going down the steps to the subway. That threw Angelo for a loop. Maybe she would throw him under the subway. However this turned out, the subway would be a quicker end.

"Anything you want to say?" Yvonne prompted.

Angelo looked at her blankly. He wondered, *If we're not going to the Eaton Centre, where is she taking me?*

"No? Nothing? You sure?"

After transferring from the subway to a bus, Angelo began to clue in. At first, it was an expensive car speeding by outside the bus window. Then it was the big trees void of their leaves. Finally, it was the large homes that came into view. Maybe Yvonne was late for work.

They exited the bus and walked down a snow-lined sidewalk.

Angelo wondered where the dog in the colourful sweater and boots was. They turned onto the driveway in front of the sprawling house with too many windows to count. The black BMW SUV with tinted windows was parked near the large garage doors.

Yvonne punched a code and the service door popped open. "Last chance, Angelo," she warned.

He shrugged. He followed her lead and removed his boots. "I didn't bring any homework to do," he said.

She threw an unpleasant look his way. "Homework? Really?"

Angelo stepped inside. The house with vaulted ceilings, marble floors, and pristine furniture was as intimidating as before. The only difference was that this time, he knew his way around.

They walked down the long hallway that opened into the large kitchen. Angelo was shocked to see the Queen herself. Mrs.

Harrington was standing there, waiting for them. Her son Jacob sat at the table.

Angelo took note that neither of them looked friendly or happy. He turned to Yvonne and said in Tagalog, "Why are we here? What's going on?"

Yvonne stood silently.

The Queen sat down, poured herself some steaming tea, and broke the silence. "Thank you for coming here." She uncrossed her hands. "We aren't coming out and accusing anyone just yet. Let's start this with just a simple question. Something has recently gone missing. Do you know anything about it?"

Angelo stared at her blankly.

The Queen made a rectangular shape in the air. "It's a hockey card."

Angelo recoiled inward, like he did when confronted with the volley of questions by mall security. Instead of a heavily ironed uniform and coffee in a white Styrofoam cup, the Queen wore shiny jewellery and was sipping tea out of a gold-rimmed cup with a matching saucer. But to Angelo, it felt the same.

Angelo looked at Jacob. He flashed back to the messy bedroom where the boy had been showing off the hockey card.

The Queen focused on Angelo. "Do you know what hockey is?"

Angelo didn't respond.

Jacob stepped in and pointed his finger at Angelo. "Where's my Gretzky card? I know you took it."

Angelo was about to mutter something when Yvonne added her voice. "Did you take it? *Kinuha mo ito?*"

"We notice when important items go missing," Mrs. Harrington said. "And it was about the same time —"

"Excuse me, Mrs. Harrington," Yvonne said. "Jacob had a friend over that day. Maybe that boy played with it."

Mrs. Harrington rolled her eyes. "That's the only excuse you have?"

"With all respect, maybe it was knocked over. There's a lot of . . ." She paused to search for a respectful word. "A lot of *stuff* in there. Let me look. Maybe I will find it."

The Queen's voice got sharper. "You don't think we looked everywhere? We turned that room upside down!"

"But the card, it's small."

She calmed. "Might be small to you. But it is hugely important to us."

"Maybe when I was cleaning, I accidentally knocked it over. Did you check —"

"Stop talking. Stop coming up with ridiculous excuses."

"Mom, I know he took it," said Jacob. "When he was here, you should've seen how he looked at me. Like he was angry or something."

Angelo felt the heat of everyone's eyes on him.

The Queen took a slow sip of tea through her red-lipstick lips. The teacup made a gentle chiming sound when it touched down on the saucer.

"Yvonne, why don't you ask your son? He's said nothing."

Yvonne nervously turned to Angelo and hesitated. He noticed her lips were bare and dry. The Queen hadn't offered her any tea.

"Angelo." Yvonne's forehead creased as she switched from English to Tagalog. "Tell Mrs. Harrington that you didn't steal the hockey card."

Angelo knew the situation was serious. But when his mom spoke to him in Tagalog, it took it to a brand-new level. He blared back in Tagalog, "I didn't do anything!"

Yvonne looked him square in the eyes. She placed her hands on his shoulders so he couldn't turn. She continued in Tagalog. "Angelo, please just tell the truth." She spoke through falling tears. "Tell her if you took it."

Mrs. Harrington hit the kitchen table with her hand. "Stop it. The both of you. Simply return the hockey card now."

Yvonne wiped her tears away. She reminded

Mrs. Harrington that they had recently hosted a big party.

Mrs. Harrington stood. "Enough! My guests are wealthy and could buy a thousand of their own hockey cards. Yvonne, you're fired."

Yvonne covered her chest with her hand. "Fired?"

"And I'll let my friends know about this. So you'll lose those jobs too."

"Please —"

"Not only that, but we will be pressing charges against your son. Get out."

As Yvonne turned, Angelo felt her pull him with her. Out of the corner of his eye, Angelo could see that Jacob was smiling.

Chapter 12

Gulo (Mess)

Tension was thick in the tiny apartment. Yvonne was fired, and Angelo was waiting for the big fight. But the moment when she let him have it never came. She didn't say anything. She just closed her bedroom door.

Angelo woke the next morning to the sound of the TV. Some ad was blaring, so he had to get off the futon and fish the control from deep under the covers to turn it down.

The first thing he noticed was that Yvonne

was gone. He knew the Queen wasn't her only job, but she was the biggest. The second thing he noticed was that there was no morning note on the table. He felt bad that Yvonne had been fired. But he argued to himself that she shouldn't have brought him to work. Sitting there all day in the kitchen while she cleaned up after the Queen, Angelo had felt unwelcome and humiliated.

Angelo zoned out of his morning class, wishing he could be on Paolo's boat. He wondered how the weather was and if the winds were bad. Weaker winds brought the fish closer to the surface.

He caught up with Felix, Darius, and Marcus at lunch.

They found a safe corner at the bottom of the staircase. Away from prying eyes, Felix extended his hand. Inside were some bills. Felix said, "Hard work is always rewarded."

Darius licked his lips. "That's a beautiful thing."

Marcus laughed.

Felix nodded. "Together, we are unstoppable." Then he distributed the wealth.

Darius flipped through the money, counting it. He didn't get too far before Felix slapped him on the shoulder.

"You think I'm gonna rip you off?"

"No," Darius replied.

"Then what are you doing?"

Darius stumbled over his words. "I don't know. You know . . ."

Angelo pocketed his take right away. As much as he wanted to do exactly what Darius had done, he didn't dare count it in front of Felix. A big part of what they were about was trust.

Darius tried to apologize.

"Don't say you're sorry," Felix said. "Just don't be so stupid."

Darius nodded and swallowed his pride.

Marcus patted Angelo on the shoulder. "Don't spend it all in one place."

"Not me," Angelo said. He kept his hand in his pocket, comforted by the feel of the bills in his hand.

He thought back to the fishing boat again. He remembered how hard he and his grandfather had worked selling fish on the dock to make half what he had in his pocket. There were poor people who would just steal the fish out of his hands. Paolo would tell them, "You cannot pull hair from the bald. Money before fish."

Some voices filled the stairwell so the boys headed toward the cafeteria. Angelo was looking forward to ordering something hot and tasty with his money. At the doors to the cafeteria, Angelo felt Marcus bodycheck him. He knocked him out of the path of the door.

Angelo started to call out, "What's that for?" Then he heard a familiar voice.

Felix was saying, "Good afternoon, Mr. Williams."

"Felix," Mr. Williams said, "you seem to be missing someone in your little entourage."

Angelo pressed his back against a wall.

"Don't know what you're talking about. It's just us."

"Have you seen Angelo?"

"No." Felix turned to Marcus and Darius. "You guys?"

They both shook their heads.

"Fine," Mr. Williams said, "be that way." He moved past the cafeteria door. But Angelo could see part of his arm as he turned back to say, "Oh, do me one favour. Tell him that I've contacted his mother. If he doesn't make himself available, I'm going to have to visit him at home."

Angelo tried to make himself invisible as Mr. Williams turned and headed in the opposite direction.

Marcus waved Angelo when he was in the clear.

Angelo asked, "Would he actually show up at my apartment?"

"No," Darius said. "This is just a dumb game of poker, and he's bluffing."

Angelo felt a little assured. "Good."

Felix put his arm around Angelo and forced him deeper inside the cafeteria. "Enough talk. I'm hungry and Angelo's buying!"

✵✵✵

Outside the Filipino Centre, Angelo saw Yvonne. Arms crossed, she said, "I'm surprised you showed."

He blew past her. "I'm surprised you're here."

"Hold on a moment."

He stopped, but didn't turn.

"Angelo, what did I ever do to you? Huh?"

Angelo tensed up and his fists clenched. "Are you kidding me? You brought me to this stupid country. I was happier in the Philippines without you."

"Angelo, it really hurts to hear you say that. Everything I've done here was for you."

"What? Working for spoiled people who treat you like garbage?"

Some people entering the centre stepped around them.

"I wouldn't have had my apartment when I moved out if it wasn't for Mrs. Harrington. I worked to get enough money for your plane ticket, for your futon, for the extra food."

Angelo's voice cracked. He couldn't tell what he was feeling. "Why?"

Yvonne's voice softened. "For a better life. For your future."

Angelo looked at Yvonne and thought about walking away. Instead, he pulled the cash from his pocket and gave it to her.

Yvonne looked at it, her eyes wide with astonishment.

"Take it, it's yours," Angelo said. "I can make money without you cleaning toilets."

"Angelo, where did you get this?" Yvonne's voice grew louder as her anger built. "Where did you get this?"

He didn't respond.

"Oh my God." Yvonne put her hand to her

mouth. "Did you steal that hockey card and sell it?"

"No, you don't understand —"

"Angelo, not only is Mrs. Harrington going to press charges, but I've lost my biggest job and soon all her friends will drop me. I'm begging you to confess to taking the hockey card. You don't know what you've done!"

"You're just like them," Angelo said, trying to sound angry. "Against me and assuming the worst." Even he didn't believe himself when he spoke.

Yvonne reached out a hand to Angelo's arm. "Whatever you've done to get this . . ." She held out the money. "I'd rather have half of what you have here and earn it the right way. I might clean homes, or toilets as you put it, but at least I do it honestly."

Inside the library of the Filipino Centre, Angelo sat steaming in a chair. He dug the sharp end of a pencil into the table in front of him, angry with himself for showing Yvonne the money. *It was a big mistake*, he thought. *What was I thinking? That she'd appreciate me helping out to make our lives easier?*

Angelo snickered at himself. At a deeper level in the bottom of his brain, a dream was hidden in some molecule. He saw himself saving up enough money so they could get their own apartment. It didn't have to be much bigger than the one they were in now, but it would be a two bedroom. Angelo would have his own space. It would be a place where he could close the door and shut out the world. He could think, listen to music, and fix it up with the money he got.

The molecule burst as the lead in his pencil snapped and his hand hit the table. It got the attention of a small group who were getting the homework help that Angelo had refused.

The group returned to their work.

Angelo shrugged off the moment and refocused on another table. A girl was in the middle of a power nap with her head down on a textbook. Next to her was a plastic container holding a few dumplings. He got up and moved in her direction. Passing her table, he lowered his right hand. He plucked a dumpling from the container and ate it.

Chapter 13

Pulisya (Police)

On his way back to his seat, Angelo spotted Yvonne at the library door. She waved him over. He paused, surprised to see his mother standing with a police officer. He approached and quickly saw that the man, who looked to be in his twenties, was Filipino. He overheard Yvonne say to the officer, "*Mahirap gisingin ang nagtutulog-tulgan.*" He realized they were talking about him. She was saying it was hard to wake up someone who is pretending to be asleep. Yvonne was calling her son lazy.

He noticed she almost smiled when she said, "Angelo, this is police officer Mendoza." If she was trying to scare him, it worked.

The policeman extended his hand.

Angelo shook the hand. He eyed the thick belt holding a notepad, flashlight, and handgun. Across the bulletproof Kevlar chest protector, the word *Police* was printed in reflective white.

"So your mother was telling me about what happened with a missing hockey card," Officer Mendoza said.

"Maybe he can help you," Yvonne added.

Angelo didn't say anything. He was shocked to be actually talking to a police officer. If the boys could see him, they'd flip out. Or maybe just laugh.

Officer Mendoza held his police hat wedged between his arm and bulletproof vest. "A big part of my job is working in this . . . *our* community . . . helping to protect it. If you didn't take the card, then you really have nothing to worry about."

Angelo knew he was trapped, so he just nodded.

"So," Officer Mendoza said, "you didn't take it?"

Angelo shook his head.

"Answer the officer with words," Yvonne said.

Officer Mendoza smiled and patted Angelo's shoulder. "He's a quiet kid. I was too at his age. Do you know who might have taken the hockey card?"

"No."

Officer Mendoza scratched at his head. "If this lady is going to follow through and press charges, you should be prepared."

Yvonne said, "Thank you for your help."

Officer Mendoza looked at Angelo. "Yvonne, do you mind if I talk to Angelo alone?"

"Okay." Yvonne stepped away.

Officer Mendoza stepped closer to Angelo. "You have it hard. I see that."

Angelo only looked up when a walkie-talkie hanging off the top of the officer's vest squawked.

"But that's not all I see. You have a chance to get educated and create a great life for yourself."

The words were just what Yvonne had said. But they sounded scarier when coming from the police officer.

Officer Mendoza paused before asking, "So did your friends put you up to this? Or were you just strapped for cash? I'm not saying you took it. But if you did, you really should return it before things get ugly."

Angelo looked at the officer, unsure of what to say.

"I've seen boys like you come and go on these streets. First, it's stealing. Then it's drugs. And then you're stealing to pay for the drugs. Young Filipino boys and street gangs go together like, as they say in Canada, peanut butter and jam." Officer Mendoza laughed.

"But I like you, Angelo. You should write down what happened that day in the house. If you're questioned, you're going to want details." Officer Mendoza reached into his pocket and pulled out his business card. "If you want to talk, here's my contact info."

Angelo took the card. He couldn't believe his bad luck.

"If you want to get into hockey, you should check out Mathew Dumba. He's the first Filipino-Canadian to make it to the NHL. He plays defence for the Minnesota Wild. I saw him against the Maple Leafs once. He's good. Anyway" — Officer Mendoza put his hand on Angelo's shoulder — "you never know, maybe we'll see each other on my streets. Stay out of trouble. Stay in school."

✳✳✳

Angelo caught a glimpse of the CN Tower from outside Union Station. Felix was finishing a cigarette.

The night before had been another quiet one with Yvonne. She had stayed in her room. Angelo had tried to watch TV and shake the feeling that he was now on Officer Mendoza's radar.

"So why are we here?" Angelo asked, pointing to the building.

"This is the end of the rainbow," Darius said, laughing. "People coming and going. Trains and buses. It's a gold mine of golden chances."

Marcus laughed.

"Oh," Angelo said, "check this out." He revealed a smart phone with a white front. It was in a see-through plastic case. "Look what I picked up."

"Where'd you get it?" Felix asked. He exhaled a cloud of smoke with the words into the cold air.

"This place I'm forced to go to —"

Marcus looked at him. "The community centre?"

Angelo nodded.

"You're bad."

Felix ripped the phone from him. "You can't keep this stuff."

"Don't worry. It can't be traced to me. There's no SIM card. Plus, I reset it."

"That's not what he's talking about," Darius said. "Whatever you do on your own comes back to us."

"I'm confused," Angelo said.

Felix talked with the cigarette hanging out of his mouth. "Everything you do belongs to us. Whatever you take comes to me. I'm the one who sells it. Then I split up the take after I get my share."

Angelo nodded. He was starting to clue in to the world he found himself a part of with these boys.

Darius repeated slowly, mouthing each syllable. "You can't keep what you take."

Felix pocketed the cell phone and Angelo said goodbye to it.

Do I have to give back the dumpling too?

Angelo wondered. He thought about why everything had to run through Felix. "You have someone who buys the stuff?"

"Now he's seeing the light," Felix said.

"Who?"

Darius and Marcus broke into a fit of laughter.

"What?" Angelo asked.

"They're laughing at your question," Felix said, "because it's none of your business. It's *my* contact. He trusts *me* to bring him good quality stuff. Without him, none of this would be possible."

"Got it," Angelo responded. "Everything goes through you."

"It's okay, you're figuring it all out. And anyway, just so you know, everything can be traced, except for cash. Cash is king." Felix flicked the cigarette butt to the ground and let it burn out. "Let's go inside and take some stuff."

Chapter 14

Nag-Aalala (Worried)

Angelo took in the high, arching ceilings of Union Station. He followed the boys down a flight of stairs and along a path. He could see they knew where they were going. They broke out into a busy area filled with people coming and going. Angelo noticed multiple screens on the walls flashing train times. The area was littered with the garbage from fast food restaurants.

Felix said, "Okay, let's break off. Together,

we look like trouble. Everyone on their own. And we meet up outside, where we came in."

Felix and Darius separated.

Marcus said to Angelo, "Don't rush into anything."

Angelo nodded and walked the edges of the space, taking everything in. He looked for possible targets. Then he realized that *everyone* was one. He was eager to strike, but anxious about acting too early just to have something. He was also scared because there were a lot of eyes.

Angelo looked down and found a used train ticket stub. He picked it up from the floor and sat at a row of seats. He checked his stub like he was going somewhere and used the chance to glance at his neighbours.

To his right was a woman in a long, white winter coat. To his left was a man in a black ski hat reading a newspaper.

With all the people in their own little bubbles, the distraction was built in. The man folded up his newspaper and left. Around him, almost everyone else was looking down at their phones.

Angelo lowered his ticket and took a big breath. He realized that people looking at him would see a young guy travelling without luggage. He reminded himself that he had to be extra careful. Patience was the key. Just like on the fishing boat. There was never a time when the fish would just jump into the boat. He'd have the net out, but he couldn't wish them into it. He had to wait until they came to him. And almost always, they did. Angelo could remember only a handful of times when they returned to shore with next to nothing. And that was because of the weather. The hurricane season ran from May to October, and was the worst time of the year. Angelo had many memories of being trapped at home because the heavy rains would wash everything away. Going out on the sea would be suicide. Many had died thinking hurricane season ended early.

Angelo remembered surviving Super

Typhoon Yolanda as a kid. It had killed many people in the Philippines and destroyed homes. The surges had swallowed anything close to land, including boats and houses. Angelo remembered Paolo telling him that their boat was destroyed. It took two years for them to find a replacement. The new boat was much smaller, but Paolo never once complained.

Angelo looked over and noticed that someone had taken the seat left empty by the man with the paper. It was an older man with a cane. He was holding a ticket and breathing heavily. At his foot was a suitcase on wheels.

Angelo bit at his bottom lip and weighed the options. *The man is probably a grandfather. How can I do it?*

On the other side of Angelo, the woman with the long winter coat was staring into space. Angelo eyed her two bags sitting next to each other. Her purse was open and he eyed a wallet. He needed a really good distraction and decided to wait for one. Finally, a train arrived and a large group of people walked by. Angelo reached down to scratch his leg. Then he moved his hand to her wallet.

A loud commotion caught Angelo's attention. It got everyone else's attention too. Angelo lifted the wallet as he stood. Through a crowd of people, he saw two policemen rushing in the same direction. Then Marcus came into view. He was on the run.

Angelo felt a tug on the purse and he looked down at the woman.

"What are you doing?"

He said, "I'm so sorry," realizing that the distraction had distracted him. He let go of the wallet and pushed past people, disappearing in the crowd. Far away from the woman, Angelo gasped when he got a glimpse of Marcus down on the ground. One policeman had his knee pressed down on Marcus's back. The other one knelt down in front of his head.

Angelo couldn't believe what he was seeing. He felt horrible for Marcus. He felt worse that he couldn't do anything to help him. Some people had their phones out, taking videos of the takedown. Angelo wished he could get them all to stop.

He scanned the crowd for Darius or Felix and came up empty.

Marcus was dragged to his feet and taken away in handcuffs.

Angelo stumbled backward in shock. He upset people as he stepped on their shoes or toppled over their bags. But he didn't care. Marcus wasn't getting a warning like Angelo had. Marcus was going to jail. Angelo knew he had to get out and to the meeting point. He needed to see the guys, but he was lost inside Union Station.

The world around him spun as he tried going in a couple of directions that didn't get him closer to getting out. He finally found an exit sign. He thrust through a pair of doors and lurched outside. He didn't care that it had started to snow or that it was cold out. He ran up the outside stairs and along the building until he spotted some of the CN Tower. Then he found the place where they had entered.

Darius stood there, waiting. When he saw Angelo, he smiled. "I did so good. Stuff's gotta be worth a thousand dollars easy, added up."

Angelo was out of breath. "They got Marcus."

"What?"

"The police. They moved quickly, jumped on him. They put him in handcuffs."

"Oh crap."

"You see Felix?"

"Nope. Just came out here when I couldn't store anything more."

"We have to help Marcus. How can we help Marcus?"

"We can't, Angelo. Not now."

"What do we do, then?"

Darius shrugged. "Get out of here. Go home."

"You kidding me? That's the plan?"

"It sucks big time that they got Marcus.

And if he gets arrested and there are charges, he'll fight it. Settle it."

"What?" Angelo screamed out.

"Cool it. You're drawing attention." Darius looked around. "I'm out of here."

Angelo was near tears on the streetcar home. He tried his best to hold it in. He just wanted to be home. *Just get home*, he told himself. *Keep it together.*

At the apartment building, Angelo took the stairs two at a time. And then he whipped open the door to the hallway and hurried into the apartment.

On his way to the futon, he spotted Yvonne sitting at the kitchen table, drinking a cup of tea. He realized she'd normally still be at the Queen's house at this time.

Angelo went straight into the bathroom and clicked the door locked. He stood in the shower. With the hot water falling on him, he tried to come to terms with what happened to Marcus at Union Station.

Chapter 15

Mga Tanong (Questions)

Two days later and there had been no sign of Marcus at school. The boys didn't get together after school. So Angelo found himself on the futon in front of the TV with the volume turned down low. Yvonne was in her room with the door closed. He hadn't realized just how much she worked at the Queen's house.

Angelo drifted off into a nap out of sheer boredom. He awoke at the sound of a knock on the front door. Before he could react, Yvonne came out of her room and walked toward the door. She said, "Get up, it might be for you."

Angelo was confused. Who would be coming to see him? He stepped to the open door and couldn't believe who was standing there.

Mr. Williams smiled and shook Yvonne's hand. "Good afternoon. Is this still a good time?"

Yvonne said yes and invited him inside.

Angelo made eye contact with Mr. Williams. He couldn't get over the shock of seeing the teacher in their apartment.

Mr. Williams removed his boots and draped his coat over the kitchen chair. Angelo was invited to join them at the kitchen table.

Yvonne asked, "Can I get you anything, Mr. Williams? Tea, a glass of water?"

Mr. Williams declined. He placed a dark red folder on the table and unclipped a pen. "I wanted to meet to create a formal pathway of communication between you, Angelo, and myself." He opened the folder and drew a large triangle on the notepad inside. "Triangles are the strongest of all the shapes because any added force is evenly spread through all three sides."

Did he come here to teach a math lesson? Angelo wondered.

"The three of us each sit at a point." He wrote an initial at each of the points. "If we maintain this strong shape — an open line of communication — it will benefit us all."

Angelo noticed Yvonne nodding. He realized that the triangle was like the way the boys had hid him from Mr. Williams.

"So let me get right to my reason for being here. Things have been difficult for Angelo at school."

Yvonne shot Angelo a disappointed look.

"But please understand that it is to be expected," Mr. Williams went on. "Students new to the school, and especially new to Canada, often have a very hard time adjusting. It's important to see things through their eyes. I can relate a little. I was born in Ghana in West Africa. I suppose I had it a bit easier because

I came to Canada when I was younger. We came because of troubles with the government. When we got here, there was a lot of racism. Even though my parents were educated, their credentials were not accepted in Canada."

Angelo sat in his chair, trying to crack his knuckles under the table. *Now it's a history lesson?*

"How are things at home with Angelo?"

"Not good," Yvonne said.

Mr. Williams nodded and sat back in his chair. "Angelo, as you find yourself making this transition, I want you to think about what your mother has done for you. How much she's given up to get you here."

"I try to explain to him," Yvonne added. Angelo could hear the frustration in her voice. Mr. Williams nodded.

"Well, as much as leaving family and coming here was your journey, this is his. It will take time."

"Such a young boy. And he has a lot of issues . . ."

Yvonne was caught in mid-thought. Angelo prayed, *Please don't bring up that stupid hockey card! Please!*

He was relieved when Mr. Williams jumped in. "Some of the issues at school have to do with the friends he's made. They are a group of boys who have lost their way."

Yvonne smacked her hand down on the kitchen table. "Angelo, you must stop seeing these boys."

Angelo stared at a line in the table.

"They might have turned away from good decisions," Mr. Williams said. "But, Angelo, I'm here to tell you that it's never too late to focus on your studies. The future here for you is wide open."

"That's right," Yvonne added.

"Do you have other family here? People he can connect with?"

"No, but we do go to the Filipino Centre."

"Excellent. I've heard amazing things about that place." Mr. Williams ripped the page with the triangle on it out of his notepad and handed it to Angelo. "We are always here for you. You are the most important part of this triangle. So, at school, please don't hide from me."

Angelo took the paper. He politely walked Mr. Williams to the door.

✲✲✲

The next few days at school were uneventful. But there was still no word about Marcus. Angelo knew that his absence from school meant it was bad. Rumours started flying around for a few days that he'd been arrested. They were only rumours, but the three boys continued to keep a distance from each other. For the first time since Angelo had met them, they weren't talking. Felix had said the less they were around each other for a few days, the better, but that it would all blow over soon. Angelo made sure he checked in with Mr. Williams. He didn't want the teacher showing up at the apartment anymore.

After school, Angelo was spending his time at the Filipino Centre. He sat in the same chair he always did. Pretty quickly, he got bored and started to scan the room for possible items he could make his. Angelo knew that stealing would get him into trouble. But he found it addictive. Plus, there was the cash that would come in from Felix, when all this was over. He felt a rush from being able to pull it off, not get caught. It made him feel powerful.

He looked around the room and saw that it was almost too easy. People were much too unsuspecting. There were no cameras.

A calculator, a mechanical pencil, and a phone charger later, Angelo walked up the stairs of the Filipino Centre. He was to meet his mom at a thrift store, where she was selling some of her clothes for cash. He opened the front door of the centre to leave as Officer Mendoza stepped inside.

"Angelo. How are you?"

A little dazed from almost literally running

into the police, Angelo muttered, "Okay."

"Any news about that hockey card?"

"No."

"Well, no news can often be good news." Officer Mendoza stomped some snow off his boots. "Hey, I'm glad I bumped into you. There was something I wanted to ask you."

"I have to —"

"Just a question and you can go. There's a guy about your age that I used to see around here. His name is Marcus. You know him?"

Angelo nodded.

"You guys probably go to the same high school, right?"

Angelo shrugged his shoulders.

"Anyway, he got caught doing something stupid. He tried to steal something and was arrested. I've been dealing with his parents. He's in a whole bunch of hot water. You might want to be careful around him."

Angelo could feel the calculator, pencil, and charger in his jacket pocket as Officer

Mendoza went on his way.

Angelo met up with Yvonne and trailed behind her on the cold walk back to the apartment. Once home, Yvonne said that she was tired and went to her room. Angelo flopped down onto the futon and searched for the remote. He found it and flicked on the TV. First the guidance counsellor, and now the cop. One thing he was sure of, he hated all the extra attention. If he finally did get caught, would an embarrassed Yvonne send him back to the Philippines?

Angelo reached down under the futon and pulled out Jacob's hockey card. He held it in his hand and examined it. He never heard the name Wayne Gretzky before. The young blond boy on the card wasn't much older than Angelo. He wore a blue and orange uniform and was skating at a steep angle while looking up. Angelo tried to figure out how he didn't fall over. He also wondered why anyone would pay a lot of money for a paper card.

Chapter 16

Gupitin (Cut)

Angelo sat in class, his foot tapping on the ground, driven by nerves. He was having a hard time focusing because the hockey card was in his pocket. He had debated whether he should bring it in or not. But the thought of Yvonne going through his clothes and finding it scared him. Plus, he really needed to sell it. Either way, he had to get it out of his room, so he brought it with him.

Lunch took forever to arrive. Finally,

Angelo headed out in search of Felix. Along the way, Mr. Williams caught him.

"Angelo!" Mr. Williams said, waving him down.

Angelo thought about making a sharp turn away, as if he hadn't seen Mr. Williams. But he'd learned that Mr. Williams was really persistent.

"Come over here." Mr. Williams curled his index finger, making what he wanted crystal clear.

Angelo stopped, hands in pockets, in front of Mr. Williams. He followed the teacher to his office.

Once the door was closed, Mr. Williams was quick to start. "Angelo, I just spoke with your mom. I was concerned that you might have been offended by my showing up at your home. Then she tells me that you're being brought up on theft charges."

Angelo didn't respond. He was cool on the outside, but inside he was burning up with rage.

"That's very scary. Having a criminal record is serious. They can stop you from leaving the country. How would you like to never go back to the Philippines?"

Angelo shuddered at the thought. The hockey card felt like it was burning a hole through his pocket.

"Plus, a university or college won't want you to study there. Getting a job will be very challenging. Think about what that would do to your mom. Angelo, are you listening to me?"

Angelo removed his hands from his pockets. They were hot and sweaty.

"You can only be quiet for so long before it catches up on you," Mr. Williams ended. "You can go now."

Angelo closed the office door on his way out. He just wanted the hockey card gone. If he could get Felix to sell it, he wouldn't be haunted by the sight of it.

Angelo didn't have to look far to find Felix

and Darius. They had eyes on him as he came out of the office.

"What did Mr. Williams want?" Felix asked. "Looked serious."

"Just giving me a hard time about my homework." Angelo looked Felix in the eyes. He didn't want to get caught lying. Felix was all he had. "And he told me not to hang with you guys. Said you were both bad news."

Felix and Darius laughed.

Angelo asked, "Did you guys hear about Marcus?"

Darius spoke first. "No."

"He's been arrested."

"There's nothing we can do about that," Darius said.

"Darius is right," Felix said. "Marcus didn't protect himself. He got caught and we can't save him."

"Should we visit him? He lives in the building next to mine."

"It won't do you any good," Felix said.

"And what are you going to say?"

"Felix is right," Darius added.

"We have to cut Marcus off," Felix explained. "Move on and keep doing what we're doing. Life don't stop because he got caught."

"That's right. Time for some change," Darius offered. "Listen to the man."

"Marcus is a good guy and still our friend," Felix said. "But what good is he to us if he can't pull in anything? Bottom line."

Angelo couldn't believe how ruthless Felix was. Friendship meant nothing. It was all about the money. In that moment, Angelo didn't want to give Felix the hockey card anymore. *Is there a way to just return it?* Angelo thought. "So that's it?" he asked.

"You want to hug it out?" Darius laughed. "Hold hands?"

Angelo held the hockey card in his hand, doing his best to cover it.

"Everyone just chill," Felix demanded. "Angelo, how did you hear about his arrest?"

Angelo hesitated before saying, "My mom."

The bell rang to signal the start of the next class. Angelo nodded his head and repeated Felix's words. "You're right. Agreed. Let's chill."

Darius laughed at him. "Chill doesn't sound chill at all when you're saying it."

Angelo shrugged off the comment and turned to his locker instead of heading to class. He felt the urgent need to get the hockey card to safety. He placed the card in its clear sleeve carefully in an empty plastic bag. He muttered, *Bihirang masilayan, agad nakakalimutan.* Something seldom seen is hopefully soon forgotten. He dropped the plastic bag into his backpack and took a long sigh. He wasn't sure what his next step should be. He thought about Yvonne, unaware of the boys standing close by, watching him.

Darius tapped Angelo's shoulder. "Angelo, you're acting weird, man."

"It's just what's happening to Marcus. It's getting to me," Angelo said.

"You're not chickening out, are you?" Felix asked.

"No."

"Then what's going on?"

"Nothing."

Darius asked, "What, you too good for us now?"

Angelo tried to keep his cool. "Yeah, you've got me. I've made friends with the Trinidadians. I work with them now."

"I knew it!" Darius said, pointing a finger at Angelo's face.

"He's messing with you, Darius," Felix said.

"So, guys," Angelo started, "when are we getting back at it? I was thinking of the Eaton Centre again. That place is huge."

"Soon," Felix said. "Not yet."

"I don't know," Darius added. "I still think he's up to something, Felix."

"I'm not up to anything, believe me," Angelo pleaded.

"I don't know . . . Darius is usually good

about this kind of thing." Felix looked at Angelo. "He can smell a rat."

Angelo responded in Tagalog. "You think I'm a rat? Angelo Tomas Torres. That sound like one to you?"

"That's your middle name?" Darius asked.

Angelo nodded. He saw Felix looking at his backpack. "What's yours?" Angelo asked, praying that Felix wouldn't look in it.

Felix reached into Angelo's locker and pulled out his backpack.

"What're you doing?" Angelo asked.

Darius answered for Felix. "Locker inspection, Tomas."

Angelo watched in anguish as Felix rifled through. *How is this happening? What did I ever do to them?* His stomach dropped when Felix pulled out the plastic bag and removed the hockey card. "Leftovers?" Darius asked.

Felix looked at Angelo angrily. "Holding back on us?"

"I was going to —"

Felix reached into the bag for the hockey card.

"Don't touch it!" Angelo begged. But it was too late.

Felix said, "What is this?"

"What do you know about hockey?" Darius asked.

Behind them, a teacher walked by. "You boys should be in class," she said.

Before Angelo could react, Felix dropped the hockey card back into the plastic bag.

"Sorry," Felix said to the teacher. "We were just helping a friend with a stuck lock."

"Just get to class, boys."

"Yes, miss," Darius said with a smile.

Angelo watched Darius go first. Felix took off in the opposite direction — with the hockey card.

Chapter 17

Natakot
(Scared)

No, no, no. This can't be happening, Angelo thought as he trailed behind Felix. He had it straight in his mind that there was no way in hell he would let Felix get away with the hockey card.

They moved through the empty hallway. Behind the closed classroom doors, lessons were being given.

"Felix. That's mine," Angelo said.

"I don't know what you're talking about."

"Stop."

Felix did. "Sure, whatever you want."

Angelo had never had the guts to stick up to a guy like Felix. And now was no different.

"Tell me what you want," demanded Felix. "Because I'm late for class."

"Since when are you interested in being on time?"

Felix's posture changed. He stood up taller and stepped closer.

Angelo extended his hand, almost touching Felix. "Give me the card."

Felix smirked. "I don't know what you're talking about."

"The card you took from my backpack."

"Oh, that."

"It's in the plastic bag. Give it to me."

"Angelo, keeping something from me was a big mistake. Why do this over a stupid worthless card?" Felix pushed Angelo backward.

Angelo recovered and put his hand out again. "You don't know the story behind that hockey card. You don't know how important it is to me."

Felix held out the plastic bag. "You into hockey now?"

Angelo reached for it and Felix swatted him away. He tried again and failed.

A voice behind Angelo rang out. "What are you two doing?"

He didn't have to turn to know it was Mr. Williams.

"You should both be in class. Now."

"Looks like your friend is here," Felix taunted Angelo.

"He's not my friend." Angelo lurched forward, trying to knock Felix down.

Felix stepped back and Angelo stumbled.

"I'm not going to ask you two again!" Mr. Williams headed toward the boys.

Felix smiled at Angelo and called out to Mr. Williams. "Right away, sir. Sorry, sir." Then Felix focused on Angelo, lowering his voice. "All Williams sees is some poor, troubled Filipino punks."

Angelo looked up at Mr. Williams. Felix's words scrambled around in his head. Confused, but angry, he reached out and grabbed Felix by the shirt. "Give it back to me!"

Felix backed up, pushing Angelo off him. "He's crazy, Mr. Williams. He's got problems."

Angelo pushed Felix hard into a set of lockers.

"Stop it!" Mr. Williams called.

Felix stepped aside and pushed through an exit door.

Angelo followed him outside. The air was cold and it was snowing.

Mr. Williams stood at the open door and screamed out, "Don't do anything, Angelo. Whatever's happening, walk away. Go back to class. Nothing's worth this."

Felix stood in the blowing snow. He smiled and asked, "What do you call two Filipinos fighting in a snowstorm?"

Angelo's answer was to jump at Felix again. He missed and fell to the cold, wet ground.

"You want the bag so badly?" Felix asked. "Here you go." He let go of it. The wind made it scurry along the ground.

Angelo quickly caught up to the bag and stepped on it. He picked it up and riffled through it. It was empty.

Felix looked at Angelo and said, "Thought you'd have learned by now. Never hang around longer than you have to."

"Get in here!" Mr. Williams yelled.

Felix tucked his hands in his hoodie pockets. He smirked. "The card's long gone, Angelo." Then he turned and walked back toward the school. "Sorry, Mr. Williams. We were arguing about who the Maple Leafs should trade. It was a guy thing. And it's over."

As Felix passed him to get inside, Mr. Williams warned, "Whatever that was, I'll see you after school."

Angelo stood in the field. Everything was a blur against the gusting snow. He slowly realized that Felix didn't have the hockey card. He had just been the distraction. At the locker, he had given it to Darius, who took off. Feeling like a fool, Angelo didn't care about the cold anymore.

I'm done, he thought. *Why did I ever take the hockey card from the apartment?* He weighed the few options he had left. Just walking away seemed like the easiest. The thought of having to face Mr. Williams after all that had happened made him feel ill.

Angelo took a step away from the school and then stopped. The apartment keys were in his jacket, which was in his locker. He ducked under Mr. Williams's arm, still holding the door open.

Angelo stepped into the warmth. He stood covered in snow.

Mr. Williams looked down at him. "Want your mother to know about his?"

Angelo didn't respond. *This* didn't mean squat compared to what was coming his way.

"Go get dried off and head back to class, Angelo. I'm following in five minutes."

*** *** ***

At the end of the school day, Angelo was still upset. *What was I thinking*, he asked himself over and over as he went down the hall, through the school doors, and out the front. He paused when he saw a police car pull up. He flipped up the hood of his jacket so it covered his face. Then he changed direction. His mind raced. *Are they here for me?* he wondered.

A voice called out after him, "Hey."

Angelo knew the voice. He turned to see Officer Mendoza standing at the car with a female police officer.

Chapter 18
Tulong (Help)

Mendoza left his partner and walked up to Angelo. "How are you doing?"

"Not good."

"I'm sorry to hear that."

"You here for me?"

Officer Mendoza laughed. "No. Well, maybe. You know that Marcus guy we talked about? I found out he wasn't alone. He was running in a gang."

Angelo broke into a frozen sweat.

"You know anything about Filipino gangs at this high school?"

Angelo nodded.

"You a member?"

Angelo said, "No." After what had just happened with Felix, it wasn't really lying.

Officer Mendoza grinned. "I appreciate the honesty. We Filipinos need to stick together." And he followed his partner into the school.

About halfway between school and home, Angelo began to see that he had no choice but to confess. The hockey card could be anywhere. By now, Felix had probably sold it to his guy and was smiling and counting the cash. And Felix had one less person he had to share the wealth with.

I've messed up big time, Angelo thought. *Confess and pay the price.*

The thought of the Queen smirking at Angelo as he confessed sent chills down his spine. The money meant nothing to her. She could probably buy a new hockey card. What would make the Queen happy was to know that she took down Angelo and Yvonne. All of her suspicions would be proven true.

He could see her saying, "If her son took the hockey card, who knows what Yvonne took over all those years? My boy Jacob and I feel so violated!"

Angelo kicked a clump of frozen snow and watched it splatter. At their building, he waited for the elevator. At their door, he slowly inserted the key and turned the knob quietly so it would not alert Yvonne. Stepping inside, Angelo took off his wet boots and socks and tiptoed to the futon. He sat in front of the television, holding his breath and listening for any sounds. Nothing but silence.

After a short shower with almost hot water, Angelo towelled off and changed into dry clothes. Minus the dripping from the shower tap, the apartment was still quiet. He stepped toward Yvonne's bedroom and pressed his ear to the closed door. There was no sound, so he opened it. He saw Yvonne's small, single bed with a small, soft plush carpet beside it. The night table didn't match the colour of the clothes cabinet. Over her bed was a wooden cross with a wire design around it.

Angelo stepped closer to her bed and then sat on it. He lifted his bare feet and lay down. It was soft, much softer than the futon. It had been a long time since he was in a bed. Staring up at the ceiling, he closed his eyes for a moment and revelled in the stillness.

He opened his eyes and found himself looking at a wall. *Did I drift off?* he wondered.

On the night table was a framed picture. Looking back at him was a much younger version of himself. Yvonne was squeezing him and their faces were pressed together closely. In the background, Angelo picked up hints of his old home. Next to the garden was a wire cage filled with birds. Angelo thought of his favourite silver pheasant with its bright-red face.

Angelo remembered how happy he was in the Philippines. He also remembered that the photo was taken just before Yvonne left. That younger Angelo had no idea that she'd be gone for years. That she would leave him sad. And then bring him to a place that made him even sadder.

He thought about the Queen smirking during his confession in front of a judge. *Maybe there was a way to get out of this.*

Angelo stood and straightened the sheets and pillows, removing his imprint. He closed the bedroom door on his way out.

If his plan was going to work, he had to move fast.

Angelo left a note for Yvonne that he'd be a little late at the Filipino Centre. He pocketed the money he had left from doing business with Felix and took the stairs, two at a time, all the way to the ground floor. He flew out the main doors of the building and turned onto a path. It led to a small courtyard that linked his building with another one. At the entrance, he scanned the directory, trying to remember Marcus's last name. He thought back to the Filipino Centre where he first met Marcus — it was Ramos.

There were families named Ramos on the third, fourth, and eighth floors. One of them had to be Marcus's apartment. It took only a few minutes for someone to exit so Angelo could grab the door and sneak in. On the third floor, he found the first Ramos apartment and knocked. The handle turned and the door opened a crack.

The door was still chained. Angelo saw an older Filipino woman looking out. She asked who he was in an agitated voice. Before he could even reply, he heard Marcus's voice. The woman closed the door in his face. He stood there, not knowing what to think. He had turned to leave when the door opened again. Standing there was Marcus.

Marcus let Angelo in. The place looked a lot like Angelo's place. There was a small kitchen and a couch with a TV. He was surprised when Marcus opened a bedroom door and invited him in.

"You have your own room?"

"Yeah. I got it when my brother went to university." Marcus sat on his bed.

"So. Why you here? Nothing you can do to change what happened."

Angelo nodded.

"Felix sent you?"

"No." Angelo snickered. "We had it out today."

"What happened?"

"It's a long story. Marcus, I really screwed up and I need your help."

"Don't know what I can do for you. I was arrested and found guilty. So there's that. I'm suspended from school. The principal is trying to connect me to some other thefts there. My parents don't trust me enough to use the washroom on my own. And that's just the start. I've got this Officer Mendoza on my case . . ."

Angelo nodded. "I know him too. He's been hanging around the Filipino Centre. Listen, it's not that kind of help I need right now."

Marcus perked up. "Now I'm curious."

"I need information. I need to know where Felix goes to sell the stolen stuff. I need to know who his guy is."

"Why would you need to know? Are you trying to mess with Felix by cutting him out? That's not a good idea. Felix will take you down."

"It's complicated." Angelo stood up. "Marcus, please."

"Angelo, that's a side of Felix's life we stay out of. But I'm glad you're here. I was stupid enough to ruin my life. You need to stop hanging with Felix and Darius."

"It's too late for that."

"It's not. Angelo, when we first met, I thought I was helping you. Cutting you a break, you know? I don't know what kind of trouble you're in now, but I'm sorry for dragging you into this mess."

"The name?" Angelo asked.

"I can't help you."

Angelo moved to the door. He had played every card he had to get the information. Hand on the knob, he turned. "It's been nice knowing you, Marcus. I know the way out."

Angelo left the apartment and walked slowly down the hall with his head low. What options did he have left?

"Angelo."

Angelo turned to see Marcus standing in the doorway of his apartment. His parents stood like watchdogs behind him.

"Everything okay?" Angelo asked.

Marcus nodded. "The place you're looking for is Paul's Pawnshop on Church Street."

"Thank you."

"Just don't get killed or anything."

Angelo smiled. "I promise."

Chapter 19

Desperado
(Desperate)

The sign for Paul's Pawnshop was lit up in red neon lights on top of a green awning. Angelo was watching the place from across the street, behind a bank of snow. He was hoping that Felix or Darius would show up. That way, he could just rip the hockey card from them before they sold it. He waited and waited. But knew it was getting late and he had no choice but to go inside.

He crossed the street at a break in traffic.

Close up, he could read the sign in the window: "Cash on the spot, guaranteed."

Briiing. A security alert signalled Angelo's entrance. On one side of the store were waist-high glass cabinets filled with rings, computers, cell phones, and cameras. Another cabinet had rows and rows of watches. There were open shelves filled with books, dolls, and other collectibles. In the back-left corner was a locked stand filled with a variety of knives.

"Can I help you?" An overweight, but muscular man stood behind the counter. He wore a baseball hat with a fish on it. Below his rolled-up sleeves were faded tattoos.

Angelo took slow breaths to try to control his nerves. "Yes, I'm looking for Paul."

The man let out a snort of laughter. "Ha ha ha. So you can read a sign."

Angelo continued, "I'm looking for something that might have been sold to you today by a friend."

"Uh-huh?"

"It's a hockey card."

The man didn't respond.

"It's a Wayne Gretzky hockey card."

"I don't know what you're talking about."

"My name's Angelo. Have you heard of Felix?"

"That name supposed to mean something to me? Because if it is, it don't."

"Please, sir. I'm almost certain that a hockey card belonging to me was brought in here. It was stolen, uh, from me. I really need it back."

"Stop rambling on. I don't know what you're talking about."

Angelo was desperate. "Did a guy my age . . . my, uh . . . come in here maybe an hour ago? Filipino?"

"A lot of people come and go. You can look around. You won't see any cards."

"Could I leave my name? Or come back and check in case anybody with a hockey card comes in?"

"It's time for you to leave, kid."

Angelo knew he'd pushed as much as he could. As he left the pawnshop, he spotted a police car stopped at the side of the road. Angelo kept walking. A quick look over his shoulder told him that the police car was keeping pace with him. *Why is Officer Mendoza following me?* Angelo wondered.

Then the lights flickered red and blue. A siren whirled twice.

Angelo's mind raced with horrifying thoughts. Officer Mendoza knew Yvonne. *Did she call him?*

At his right side, the police car inched by. The window rolled down. The cop in the passenger seat called out, "You going to stop?"

Angelo was surprised. It wasn't Officer Mendoza. He pointed at himself. "Me?"

"Yes, you."

The police car parked, curbside. With flashing lights still on, two cops got out of the car.

Angelo froze.

As they neared Angelo, the cop who had stopped him said, "What's your name?"

Angelo's mouth dried up. He couldn't speak.

"What's your name?"

Angelo lowered his head and forced back tears. He didn't know how much longer the dam would last before the flood broke through.

"Can you hear me?"

Angelo nodded. *Do they know Officer Mendoza?* he wondered.

"I'm going to ask one more time, pal. Your name?"

"Angelo."

The police officer smiled like Angelo had won a prize. "There you go. You got a last name to go with that?"

"Torres."

"Well, Angelo Torres, my name is Officer Jones. This is my partner, Officer Chandra. We're wondering what a kid your age is doing coming out of a pawnshop."

Angelo didn't know how to answer without getting himself in even more trouble.

"You have a record? We look up your name, we going to find anything?"

Angelo shook his head. "No, sir."

"Come over here." Officer Jones guided Angelo toward the hood of the police car. "Mind if I search you?"

Angelo shook his head, his insides nothing but burnt ash.

"You have any sharp objects on you? Needles?"

"No." Then Angelo remembered the cash in his boots.

Officer Jones had Angelo spread his hands on the hood of the police car and separate his legs. He used his gloved hands to search Angelo, pulling out a key from his jacket pocket. As the hands continued down, Angelo became more and more worried about the cash bulge in his right boot. He felt a sense of relief when Officer Jones stood and turned him around. Angelo had packed the cash well.

"Just a key on you. Were you selling or buying over there at Paul's Pawnshop?"

"No. Just looking."

"Looking?" Officer Jones looked at his partner.

Chandra replied, "Likely story."

Officer Jones held up the key and placed it in Angelo's hand.

"Can I go home?" Angelo asked.

"Yes, but first come with me."

Officer Chandra went back to the cruiser. Angelo followed Officer Jones toward Paul's Pawnshop. He held the door for Angelo before following him in.

The electronic alert went off and Paul entered from the back room. "Well, good evening, Officer." The look on Paul's face was anything but polite. "What can I do for you?"

Officer Jones started. "This young man was in your store twenty minutes ago?"

"That's right. Told him he should be home doing homework."

"Was he selling?"

"No, he was looking to buy," Paul said. He pointed. "He was looking at this little TV. Said he'd come back when he had the money. I said I'd do my best to hold it for him."

Officer Jones said, "He's too young to be shopping here."

Paul smiled. "That's exactly what I told him. What's a high school kid doing in a place like this? I told him while the deals might be good here, maybe he'd be better off shopping at Amazon or Best Buy or something like that."

"You see him in here before?" Officer Jones asked.

"No sir. Never."

Officer Jones looked at Angelo, assessing him. "Well, young man, I think it would be in your best interest to not stray this way. Understand?"

Angelo nodded.

Officer Jones moved to the exit and held the door for Angelo.

Paul quietly warned Angelo, "I'm going to tell you what I told your friend today. You try to come back in and there's going to be trouble."

"Today?" Angelo asked, smiling.

"Yeah, I'm done with you all. Why you smiling?"

"No reason." Angelo turned and passed the police officer on his way out. When he hit the sidewalk, he kept moving, walking as fast as he could.

Chapter 20

Iligtas (Save)

"Angelo, Mrs. Harrington won't let this go. Only you can end this. Give back the hockey card or confess and say you're sorry."

Angelo only half listened. His mind raced out of control in a hundred different directions.

"If you apologize, maybe Mrs. Harrington will show some sympathy for you."

He was busy planning his biggest, most dangerous theft ever. Pulling it off would take a real miracle. The kind of miracle Paolo talked about the day he caught the largest fish he'd ever seen. When Paolo had reeled it in, he raced to shore to show it off.

"Maybe she'll drop the charges. I could find a way to repay her."

If he could pull off this last theft by some miracle, he'd never take anything from anyone ever again.

"Do the right thing."

He'd have to use everything Felix had taught him.

"Officer Mendoza said that we should find a lawyer."

The timing and location had to be exact.

"And that's going to cost a lot of money."

The kind of plan he had in his mind had no back door. There was no escape once it got going.

"We're barely making it through the month as it is."

He had to commit to it.

"Say something."

Angelo looked up at Yvonne. "I'm sorry."

"While I'm glad to hear that, your apology is to the wrong person."

***

Angelo fidgeted in his seat, counting down the seconds to the end-of-day bell. When it finally rang, he was first out the door and into the hallway. He spotted Felix and Darius on their way outside and quickly chased them down.

Outside was cold, but the sun was out. Students emptied out of the school.

"Hey, Felix," Angelo called out.

Felix stopped and turned. Darius too.

"I gotta ask you something."

"Watch him come crawling back," Darius said.

Felix replied, "Too late for that."

Angelo stepped closer to Felix.

Felix tensed up, hand in fists. "So what do you want?"

Angelo dropped to his knees. "Please give the card back!"

Darius was the first to crack up.

"I need it back." Angelo pressed his hands together like he was praying. He screamed out, "Please!"

His words caught the attention of other students. Most stopped to check out the scene. Some even had their phones out, recording it.

"You got problems?" Darius said.

"I'm on my knees begging you for the hockey card back."

"How do you know I didn't sell it?" Felix asked.

"Don't get mad. But I went to Paul's Pawnshop."

"What? How?" Felix yelled.

"I followed you there yesterday."

"That kind of stupid could get you killed."

"He told me he wasn't buying anymore."

Felix took in the crowd, realizing that the scene was being recorded.

"Come on, Felix," Darius said. "He doesn't know what he's talking about."

Felix got down on his knees and lowered his voice. "You think something like that's going to stop me?" He patted his pocket and smirked. "I already have a new buyer. I'm going online."

Darius called out, "Your stupid card will be gone today!"

"Thank you for bringing me the card." Felix showed Angelo a picture of it on his phone. "It's worth at least two thousand dollars!"

Angelo gawked at it.

"It's a pretty big score. Too bad you won't get your share."

Darius jumped in with "That's right!"

Angelo reached out, but Felix got up and stepped back. Angelo went for him again, grabbing hold of his pant leg. Down on the ground and covered in slush, he called out, "Please! Please!"

At first, Felix had a hard time kicking Angelo off.

Darius laughed and called out to the crowd. "You guys getting this loser?"

A bigger kick, and Angelo couldn't hold on. He rolled a couple of times before coming to a stop. He stayed there on the ground, whimpering.

Felix took off. Darius as well. But only after shouting to someone to post the video on YouTube.

Angelo was slow to get up. He brushed off some of the slush before limping away. The crowd quickly fizzled. Angelo lingered to create some distance between him and the boys. Then he moved quickly off the school grounds, ignoring the pain in his leg where Felix had kicked him.

He crossed the street just as the light counted down and slid into a bus shelter.

A boy sitting in the shelter turned to him and said, "That was awesome! You on the ground, pulling on Felix's leg . . . and Darius was clueless."

"You were great, Marcus. They didn't see you coming."

"It was the beginning that was great. You down on your knees . . . Who does that? He didn't see me coming. What a perfect set-up."

"Any minute Felix is going to realize that the hockey card in his pocket is a regular old piece of cardboard!"

Marcus laughed. "Let them split the profit from that!"

Angelo laughed. Marcus handed him the hockey card.

Angelo held it steadily in his hand. "Can't believe I got it back. I can't thank you enough, Marcus. You risked being on school property. I couldn't have done this without you. *Ang matapat na kaibigan, tunay na maaasahan.*"

Marcus nodded. "'A true friend will always stand by you.' My parents used to say that to me. But now, I finally understand it. Like

I said, I felt horrible getting you involved in all this. I owed you this much. Plus it was awesome stealing from Felix. Using his own tricks on him."

Angelo admired the hockey card again before placing it safely in his pocket.

"I really have to go. If I don't get home before Yvonne, I'm a dead man."

Marcus nodded and the boys shook hands.

"Later," Marcus said.

"Later," Angelo replied before racing off to the subway.

Chapter 21

Magdasal (Pray)

Angelo stepped off the bus and into the serene neighbourhood of the Queen. Everything was different here compared to their place on Parliament Street. Everything was quiet. The snow was still white and fluffy. It looked like a winter wonderland. Angelo made a path of footprints as his boots crunched down into the freshly fallen snow.

Over the last little while, Angelo had done a lot of different things. He had learned new things. Today, he was learning something else. Taking the hockey card had caused him only pain. First, Angelo thought the hockey card would be forgotten. Then he thought he'd get Felix to sell it and get a nice bit of cash. It would be his greatest score and secure his spot with the boys.

How foolish, Angelo thought as he turned from the sidewalk onto the Queen's driveway. He was glad to see the snow on the driveway had been cleared and there were no cars in the driveway. Perhaps this would be his lucky day.

Angelo stepped guardedly toward the house. He went to the maid's door and gingerly punched his birthday into the keypad. It beeped and flashed red. Angelo stepped back, horrified by the idea that he wouldn't be able to do this.

Breathe, he told himself. *Breathe and calm down.*

Angelo extended his finger and tried inputting his birthday again. This time, he remembered he had to hit a small button on the top of the pad with a picture of a key on it.

The door whirred as it unlocked. Angelo twisted the handle and stepped inside. He was greeted by warmth and brightness from the pot lights in the ceiling. He closed the door and froze, listening for any sound.

Hearing nothing, he slipped off his boots. He removed the hockey card in its clear sleeve from his pocket. The floor tiles felt warm under his feet. Trying to remember the plan of the main floor, he moved toward Jacob's room.

Angelo couldn't help but wonder what would happen if he got caught. How would he explain what he was doing to the police? *Yes. I stole the hockey card. I realized it was a mistake and I was trying to return it.* If questioned why he didn't just give it back, he'd explain how that would make him guilty. Despite the fact that he was now breaking and entering a house.

He slowed past the kitchen and paused, listening for any activity. Another step and he recoiled. He heard a sound. It grew louder and he could tell it was Jacob's voice. He wasn't alone.

Angelo looked down the long hallway, past the washroom to Jacob's room. He worried he couldn't make it there and back in time.

The voices were growing louder. The boys — yes, more than one — were on the move! Angelo took cover below a half-wall. He stiffened as Jacob and at least one other friend passed by.

Angelo breathed carefully through his nose. The slightest sound would give him away. He knew he didn't have long. The boys could easily swing by again without a moment's notice.

Down in a squatting position, an idea hit him. He needed to dump the hockey card. He had to come up with a logical place, fast.

Angelo noticed that Jacob and his friends had dropped their boots and jackets on the floor. *Pigs*, Angelo thought. No wonder they needed Yvonne — someone — to clean up after them.

Angelo moved toward the front door and stopped at the jackets. *What a perfect spot*, he thought. But which was Jacob's? That was when he saw headlights reflect off the frosted glass doors. Time was running out.

Angelo picked up the first jacket. It was blue with an attached hood. He unzipped both pockets. There was nothing in either one to tell who owned it. The next jacket was white with a red stripe. Again, both pockets were empty.

The cars light were switched off. Angelo heard the sound of a door closing. He had to think fast.

How could all this come down to a gamble? My future has bad odds, he thought.

The sound of heeled boots echoed toward him.

Angelo put the red jacket down. He was about to abort the mission when he saw a tag on another one. It was like a beacon, shining in the night.

Blue Mountain Ski Lift.

Angelo recalled the Queen talking about a ski vacation over a long weekend. He slid the hockey card into the pocket and zipped it. Then he back-stepped all the way to the maid's door.

He shoved his feet into his boots. He stopped breathing at the sound of the front door opening.

The Queen mumbled her discontent at the jackets and boots strewn all over the entrance. She called out to the boys to clean up.

That's when Angelo opened the door and escaped. He was out, but the thirty metres from the door to the sidewalk were terrifying.

Angelo stepped swiftly along the edge of the driveway. Fortunately, the SUV blocked the sight of him from the front door.

Angelo performed a small celebration dance when he made contact with the sidewalk. He celebrated again when the house was well behind him. Angelo felt like a different person. A weight had been lifted off his shoulders.

No more lawyers, no more police . . .

He slowed at a corner when a police car cruised by. Angelo would have dived into a bush if he could. But it was too late. Eye contact had been made. Angelo had been identified:

Seventeen-year-old male.

Shabby clothes.
Scruffy looking.
South East Asian descent.
Criminal activity likely.

Angelo imagined them searching their database for any Filipino male on their hot list.

He prepared for another takedown and body search as the police officer in the passenger seat raised his hand.

Run, Angelo, run!

The officer waved.

It took Angelo a moment for his brain to compute the gesture. It took another moment for him to wave back. Angelo smiled as the cruiser made a left turn and went on its way.

You're the luckiest Filipino out of the Philippines, Angelo thought. Then he heard his name.

"Angelo."

He stopped and turned. Not in a million years would he have expected to see the person staring back at him.

Yvonne.

Chapter 22

Mataas Na Damdamin (High Emotion)

"What are you doing here?" Angelo asked in a high squeaky voice.

Yvonne said, "I'm here because you are here."

She looked small, even lost, against the large homes.

"Angelo, you stole Jacob's hockey card."

Angelo looked away. The thick snowflakes were still falling slowly.

"My son, when are you going to stop

ignoring me? When are you going to stop looking away?" Yvonne's voice was breaking under the weight of her feelings. "When are you going to talk to me?"

"When are you going to admit that you abandoned me?" The words left Angelo's mouth before he knew he was going to say them. Tears swelled and his heart felt heavy.

"I never did that."

"You must have hated me. You left me. For this? This is the life you wanted me to have? You could have stayed."

"It was hard for me."

"You know what I used to think? What kept me up at night? What if something happened to you? Like Dad. What if I never saw you again?" Tears escaped and ran down his cheeks. "Do you know what it was like when you were gone? Do you know what it was like . . . to stop . . . to stop thinking about you?"

The words kept spilling out. "There were times I thought, like on my birthday or

Christmas, you would show up and surprise me. There were times when you were busy and forgot to call and I thought you were dead."

Yvonne put her hand on Angelo's arms.

"You got me all excited when you came to Canada," he said. "I thought that maybe one day very soon, I'd get to join you here. But one day took too long." Angelo pulled away. "I am not the same person you sold that dream to."

Yvonne nodded. "I'm so sorry."

"I had a life back home. One that you ripped me from. And what about Paolo? Now he's got nobody. We should be with him."

"I know. I know."

Then the two stood in silence.

Angelo had said a lot. All that he had been holding in. But he didn't feel better after saying it. His heart still felt heavy. He had a lump in his throat. He didn't want to hurt Yvonne, but he had to speak the truth. The kind of words that couldn't be said from thousands of kilometres away over Skype.

"Just because this place is good for you doesn't mean it's good for me."

"Angelo, I'm sorry for all that and more. But I did what I thought was best for us . . . for you. This place may not seem like much now, but we're not the first Filipinos to come to Canada. I've met and talked to so many people who have set up a great life here. A life we couldn't even dream about in the Philippines."

Angelo listened, but didn't respond.

"A future that wasn't possible for you back home. All I'm asking and all I've ever asked is that you give it a chance."

"I'm just a punk thief."

"No, you're not." Yvonne extended her hand to Angelo's face. "You're my wonderful and talented son." She wiped away his tears. "I am so proud. *Pinagmamalaki kita.*"

Angelo smiled. It felt good to hear her say she was proud of him.

"Angelo, I am the adult. I'll do my very best to take care of us. It's not your job to do that. It's not your job to bring in money. It's your job to try, to learn, to take chances, to find yourself, to grow into the very special young man that you can be."

Angelo felt both her hands on his face.

"To become the highest version of you. That's what I need . . . that's what this world needs."

Angelo said, "*Kung may tinanim, may aanihin.*"

"That's right. If you plant something, it will come. It will harvest."

Angelo nodded. "'Whatever you do, think about it seven times.' Paolo used to say that all the time."

They both turned when they heard a small dog bark. A man was walking a dog. Angelo noticed the dog wore a colourful sweater with matching boots.

Angelo and Yvonne shared a laugh as the man excused himself and the dog while they squeezed by on the sidewalk.

Then Yvonne reached in for a hug. Angelo hugged her back. He felt like he had his mom back for the first time since saying goodbye to her in the Philippines. He felt like the little boy he once knew.

✱✱✱

At school the next day, Angelo did his best to keep to himself. He blocked out the stares and snickers when people recognized him from the videos of him begging posted online. Angelo felt it was totally worth it. He passed by Marcus's locker and sighed, counting down the days until his friend returned.

There was still no call or knock on the door from the Queen announcing that they'd found the hockey card. Charges were still going to be pressed. The only difference was that Angelo and his mom were no longer worrying about it. In a weird way, she was proud of him for returning the hockey card, even though the family didn't know it yet.

Angelo spotted Felix as he walked down the hallway. He had been able to dodge him for a few days, but he knew there would be a time when he'd have to face him.

"There you are," Felix announced.

Angelo kept moving toward a certain door. But Felix stopped and blocked his way. "I know what you did. You took the hockey card from me."

"I begged you to give it back to me. I embarrassed myself in front of everyone and you refused. My mom lost her job because of that card."

"I don't care. That hockey card was worth at least two thousand dollars. Pay me half now or you're a dead man."

They were there, at the door. Mr. Williams leaned in the doorway, arms crossed. "A threat like that needs to be reported to the principal."

Felix turned.

"It will go on your file, Felix."

Felix turned back to Angelo, frustrated, before bolting away.

Mr. Williams unfolded his arms. "How are you doing today, Angelo?"

"Good."

"Nice to hear. Get that science paper in?"

"Still working on it."

"Good to hear. Want to come in and talk about what just happened?"

"Sure," Angelo said. He followed Mr. Williams into his office.

Chapter 23

Simula (Beginning)

Angelo exited the apartment building with his mom. Bundled up and moving along the busy sidewalk, she said, "Days like today, I miss the warm blue skies of back home. I miss the mango trees and the salty air from the ocean."

"Me too," Angelo replied. "Even those days that are so hot you could feel the wetness in the thick air. And you'd know what was coming in the early afternoon."

"Warm rain." His mom nodded. "I'd go

out into it and it felt so good."

Angelo just nodded back and stepped over a slush puddle.

"You know, Angelo, there's something I never told you. I didn't want to get your hopes up. And I guess, I'm glad I did that."

"What?"

"About three years ago, I had saved enough money for a trip home."

"Really? What happened?"

"My roommate at the time took off. She went to Dubai or somewhere for work and stuck me with having to pay her rent money. We had just signed a full-year lease. It took me four months to find a new roommate. And that money was the airline ticket."

Angelo thought about how amazing it would've been if his mom had come home . . . for his birthday or Christmas.

"So," his mom went on, "I was thinking that maybe we could start a new fund. Start saving for a trip to the Philippines. Together."

"That would be awesome!"

Behind them, two brief honks sounded, then a firing of headlights. It happened again before it caught their attention.

Angelo turned to see the black BMW SUV. *What is the Queen doing in this part of town?* Angelo asked himself. *She here to deliver legal documents?*

His mom mumbled, echoing his thoughts. "What could she want?"

Angelo wasn't really that surprised by her visit. He had wondered if the hockey card would ever be found. But he knew that he could be charged for stealing the card, even though he gave it back.

The SUV came to a stop. The car window glided down, revealing the Queen behind huge sunglasses. She said, "I called. I was hoping to catch you."

Through the darkly tinted back window, Angelo could see an outline of Jacob. He seemed to be head down on his phone.

Angelo and Yvonne looked at Mrs. Harrington blankly.

"It's funny," the Queen started. "We can't exactly explain what happened with the hockey card. You know, the one from Jacob's room?"

Angelo couldn't believe she felt she had to clarify which hockey card she was talking about.

Yvonne was direct. "Why are you here?"

"The hockey card turned up in Jacob's jacket pocket. When he got home from school yesterday, he showed me and there it was." She smiled.

Angelo was relieved, but in no mood to celebrate.

There was silence for a bit before the Queen said, "So, Yvonne, I'm offering you your job back."

"Thank you," Yvonne said. "But no thank you."

Angelo was just as surprised as the Queen. "What? Why?" he sputtered.

"I have a new job," said his mom. "Thank you, Mrs. Harrington. Goodbye." She waved and walked away with Angelo.

Angelo couldn't believe it. "Hold on. You got a new job?"

His mom smiled and pointed. "Yup. At the

Filipino Centre. I'll be working the front desk to start. But there will be chances to move up."

"Wow, Mother. Amazing."

She stopped. "Did you just say what I think you said?"

Angelo paused. He had been thinking it, but this was the first time the word *mother* just slipped out. He nodded. "Yes."

She brushed a snowflake from his cheek. "It's so nice to have you back, Angelo." As they crossed the road at the light, she admitted, "I have you to thank."

"Me?"

"If it wasn't for you, I would still be working for . . . what do you call her?"

Angelo said, "The Queen."

"Well, she may be that. But she was also very good to me. Working for her allowed me to become a resident of Canada. It allowed me to bring you here."

Angelo smiled and held the door for his mother. They were surprised to see Officer

Mendoza waiting there.

"I've been looking for you, Angelo," he said.

Angelo's stomach dropped. *What now?* he thought. *It can't be the hockey card. Did he find out I was in the gang with Marcus and Felix? Is that what he's going to charge me with?*

Officer Mendoza handed Angelo a brochure. "This is for you."

Angelo took the pamphlet and unfolded it, with his mother looking on. He read the Toronto Police logo on the top. *Is this an arrest warrant?* he wondered. "What is this?" he asked.

"It's a program called the Youth Corps. We need volunteers. I figured, if you're going to graduate high school, you'll need the volunteer hours."

"That's right," his mom said.

"You can help out in the community," explained Officer Mendoza. "We have info fairs all over the place, like at the Eaton Centre."

Angelo covered his smile. "Really?"

"Yeah, and there are some barbecues

starting in a few months. You know how to flip a burger?"

"You want me to help?" Angelo asked.

"I'm sure he can learn to flip a burger," his mom said with a smile.

"You'd be helping out me and your community too. It's hard to find people you can trust, and I think you'd be perfect for the program. Promise me you'll think about it."

His mom jumped in quickly. "Oh, he will!"

Angelo nodded and said quietly, "I really appreciate this."

"No problem. Us Filipinos need to stick together."

Angelo returned a half-smiled, feeling like he didn't deserve this. Especially not from a police officer.

Officer Mendoza asked, "Is everything okay?"

Angelo glanced at his mom and then back. "There's something I have to tell you . . ."

Acknowledgments

So much goes into making a book and I would not have been able to complete it without the support from the people around me.

I'd like to start by thanking my family. Naomi, you are extremely patient with me when my head is in a book and my mind in a character. Your understanding when I needed an extra moment to get one more idea down is greatly appreciated.

A very special thank you to the Macusi family, especially Jean for your time in helping me better understand life in the Philippines. And also for helping translate from English to Tagalog.

Thank you to Tintin D.L.C. for your assistance in helping me with all things Filipino. Your assistance was invaluable in building the Filipino content, traditional phrases and adding a young adult's perspective on what it's like to be in Angelo's shoes.

Thank you to the entire Lorimer team. To my editor Kat Mototsune, thank you again for your guidance during each of the drafts. *Cold Grab* is a better book and Angelo a deeper character than when I started because of you.